~~MERRY~~ *Creepy*
CHRISTMAS

12 Twisted Tales

2O24

FROM BLACK MARE BOOKS

ii

Creepy Christmas 2024: 12 Twisted Tales

Black Mare Books

First Edition 2024

ISBN: 978-1-959008-45-3

Creepy Christmas 2024: 24 Horror Days

©2024 by Black Mirz Books. All rights reserved.

Black Mirz Books

Third Edition 2024

ISBN: 978-1-959008-45-3

CONTENTS

CONTENTS

Reunion
By Artemis Greenleaf

"THEY told me you were dead."

Ethan Allerton's father sighed. "I thought it was for the best."

"For you, maybe." Ethan launched himself from the rustic chair and stalked around the cabin.

There was no electricity, but battery-powered lamps brightened the room. A fire crackled in the wood stove, and it was almost too warm in the kitchen. The ceiling was unusually tall for a log cabin in the woods. A miniature Christmas tree sparkled with metallic ornaments on the table. By all appearances, it should have felt like being inside the picture on a holiday card.

Ethan raised his arm as if to knock the tiny Christmas tree to the floor, but stopped himself with a huff.

Robert slowly shook his head. "I know it's not the same as being there, but I did set up a fund to make sure you had everything you needed."

Ethan turned and grabbed the steel bars of the cage. "I needed *you*! But you clearly had other priorities."

Robert dropped his chin to his chest and was silent for several moments. "I'm sorry. I know you don't understand. But you will. I had hoped that my brother—"

"Could take up the slack? Fill in because you didn't care enough to raise your own son? Uncle Bas is a far better man than you, so at least I had him to turn to."

"I get that you're hurt and angry. But it's complicated. You don't know the whole story."

"You think I'm so angry I'd kill you?" Ethan clenched his jaw. "Is that why you're hiding in there?"

"What time is it?"

"What?" Ethan tilted his head.

"What time is it?"

With an exasperated groan, Ethan tapped his watch. "8:06."

"In three minutes, the moon will rise." Robert closed his eyes and pulled in a deep breath, then let it out slowly. "I feel it coming. It hurts. Everything hurts. I won't tell you not to be afraid. You should be. You can call Sebastian to come sooner than the two hours you agreed to if you want. He'll only be twenty minutes away at the truck stop. He's probably not even at the end of my driveway yet. But don't go outside until he arrives."

"What is this bullshit? You're already trying to get rid of me?"

"Of course not. I'm just giving you options." Robert lunged at the bars where Ethan stood, causing his son to jump back. "Remember this: I am *not* to be trusted. No matter what you hear, no matter what you see, do not attempt to unlock this door."

"Okay, Robert. You are creepin' me out now."

In answer, his father groaned and doubled over in pain. "Your watch is slow," he wheezed.

The older man went to his knees, then all fours. He convulsed as if he were retching, then stretched his head up and arched his back.

Ethan wrinkled his nose as the room filled with the stench of sulfur and wet dog. He covered his ears as bones cracked and Robert cried out in pain. His body elongated and swelled. His fingers and toes lengthened and sprouted vicious claws. Thick, white-tipped grey hairs ruptured from Robert's skin and grew three inches in just a few seconds.

Robert growled, a low rumble deep in his chest that Ethan felt as much as heard. Ethan backed away, then tripped over a dining chair and fell flat on his butt. He panted in terror. His father paced behind the bars. He'd gone from a 6'4" man to a wolf-human monstrosity that towered over 9' tall.

"This," Robert snarled, his voice now gravelly and at least an octave deeper. "*This* is why."

"I'm sorry! I'm sorry!" Ethan squeaked as he crawled under the table.

The front door burst open, and another monstrous wolf-man bounded inside. This one was the cinnamon and tan of a coyote. A knotty scar crossed from forehead to cheekbone across its empty left eye socket. The thing raised its snout and sniffed the air. "Where is he?"

"Nobody here but me, Axel."

"Liar!" The cinnamon wolf destroyed the distance between the door and the cage in three strides and foolishly tried to grab Robert through the bars.

Robert pounced, snatching one of the intruder's hairy wrists with his hand and the other in his teeth. Bone ground against bone and the wrist snapped. Axel roared in pain. Robert didn't let go.

Ethan gathered his wits and fled out the open cabin door. Axel might not have seen him, but his feet crunching through the ice-crusted snow were loud enough for even a mere human to detect.

"Let me go!" Axel growled.

"No, Axel. Your fight is with me. You leave Ethan out of this."

"All's fair in love and war!" At the word 'war,' Axel jerked the arm held in Robert's mouth hard enough that the bloody stump came free.

Robert spat out the severed hand and moved to clamp his considerable jaws on the other wrist, but Axel wriggled loose. With a wicked laugh, he loped out the door, a trail of blood dripping behind him.

In his rage, Robert tried to break the biometric lock, which recognized neither the werewolf retina pattern nor the fingerprint. Hurling himself against the bars for an hour and a half, he was battered and bruised when Sebastian arrived.

"Where's—"

"Go! Axel is after him!"

Sebastian raced after Ethan and Axel, guided by a bright red trail.

Robert let himself into Sebastian's house without knocking. "How's the patient?"

Ethan, who was reclining on the couch, one leg in a cast and one arm bandaged, shrank away from his father.

Robert stopped and took a few steps back. "Do you understand why I wanted you to think I was dead?"

Ethan nodded, a quick juddering up and down.

"This is me for the next twenty-eight days. I'm sorry you had to see… that part of me, but you wouldn't have believed me if you hadn't. Now, tell me what happened with Axel."

Ethan hugged a throw pillow against his chest. "I didn't know where to go, so I just ran into the woods. I climbed a tree, but he jumped up onto the limb I was on and dragged me back down. My leg's broken."

"I'm sorry that happened. Did he… do anything else?"

Ethan squeezed the pillow harder. "He got right in my face—his breath stunk so bad it nearly knocked me out—then he growled the word 'April,' and grabbed my arm. He bit me and ran off. I wanted to go home, but Uncle Bas said you and I had to talk."

Robert bowed his head. "If I had known he'd gotten wind of your visit, I would have canceled. Now he's your father as well."

"What does *that* mean?"

"To survive a werewolf bite is to join the shifter clan. He is the one who infected me. I took his eye, though."

"I wish he'd killed me."

"Ethan. Don't talk like that. It isn't—"

"It cost you your family. Now I'm a freak, too."

"Well. You can come stay with me once a month."

"Great. Now I know how Mom feels when she talks about 'the curse.'"

Robert snorted. "A cycle is a cycle. I guess."

Ethan relaxed his grip on the pillow. "What does 'April' mean?"

"It happened in the spring. Sebastian and I were out in the woods, camping. You couldn't have been older than two. Sebastian was cooking the trout he'd caught for our dinner, and I was in the trees cutting a little more firewood. Twilight had snuck up on me and it was dark before I turned back to the campsite. I smelled that putrid wet dog/sulfur reek before I picked up any sound. Something huge ambushed me and grabbed my arm in its teeth. I thought it was going to pull it out of my shoulder, so I dropped the wood and hit it in the face with the hatchet blade. The thing was so close it was hard to get a good strike, but it was enough to escape. I learned later that his name was Axel. We've had run-ins ever since."

"Whoa." Ethan sat up. "Is there any way to break this curse?"

"There is, but it won't be easy. Three of his children must each stab him with a silver blade. If he falls from those three wounds, then they must burn his body on a fire made of cedar, juniper, and ash wood. The ashes must be mixed with wolf's bane, mistletoe, and mullein, then buried in consecrated ground."

"How many... of us... has he created, Dad?"

"A lot. Most of them embrace the wolf, though. I only found one other victim who wanted to do anything about Axel. Until now."

Ethan sat up taller and smiled.

FLAP

By Artemis Greenleaf

A SCRATCHING in the box drew my attention.

A woman and her stall were set back some small way into the alley from the high street. Long afternoon shadows bathed the passage in gloom. Something was moving inside a wooden crate upon her table. Buoyed by the prospect of puppies, I hurried to her booth. A little dog would be just the thing for my young nephew, whose Christmas present I had despaired of finding, even with all the marvelous things London merchants had on offer.

"Good afternoon, madame." She did not wear the rough linen of the country folk, and I caught glimpses of black silk beneath her fine woolen cloak with each frigid breath of wind. Unless I missed my guess, her family had the ill fortune of inheriting a title, but little money to go with it. "Have you live animals there?" I gestured to the box. "I find myself in the market for a pet."

"I do not traffic in mere pets, sir. What I have are unique and valuable companions."

Perhaps she is mad, rather than impoverished. "Show us then."

Purring came from within the crate as she reached for the lid. *Not kittens. Please, not kittens. My brother-in-law cannot abide cats.*

"Bear in mind, they are very young. Rest assured, they will grow considerably." She removed the top.

Inside were two lizards, scarcely larger than the palm of my hand. One was a stunning turquoise, the other as dark and glistening as onyx. They must be some exotic reptiles from distant shores. I'd seen many an odd creature during my deployment to India, don't you know? What I didn't understand was how she'd affixed tiny wings to their backs. An obvious chicanery.

"They are the last two I have. Only hatched a fortnight past. Dragons. From the Carpathian Mountains."

I barely restrained my laughter. *Did she suppose I'd be hornswaggled with such a preposterous tale?* "Dragons, you say? Madame, do you take me for a—"

The blue dragonlet unfurled its wings and flew up. The woman deftly caught it and held it fast. It hissed and growled in protest.

"… fool." I gaped like a snared eel.

"She's a bit advanced for her age. But her brother shall soon catch her up. They grow fastest upon a diet of sheep's liver, but a chicken's will suffice."

I was not convinced that she was peddling actual dragons. However, the creature would have been unable to fly on false wings. Perhaps I should purchase them both and have them examined at the London Zoo. Their recently opened reptile house is all the rage these days. I could picture the brass plaque now: "New World Wonders! On loan from Major General Payton Deadmane"

"Sir?"

"Forgive me, madame. I find myself at quite a loss with the wonder of these… baby dragons. What size do they attain? How long-lived?"

"The Carpathians tend toward the larger side. No less than a rod tall, either of them, but not more than twenty feet. And need you ask about their life span? It is well known that dragons live to such an age as to pass out of all memory of even entire families."

Unbidden, my eyebrow arched above its twin. "And where should I keep such pets? In my stables? On a chain in the back garden?"

"Do not mock me, sir. One does not keep dragons as pets. Care for them when they are young, and they must surely imprint upon you—favorable or not, depending on your treatment—and, if they are well disposed toward you, will come to your aid when you are in peril. They might also advise you on financial matters, but not all are amenable to doing so."

I raised my hand to touch the tiny blue dragon. What I presumed was a tongue flicked out and struck my finger. I yelped, and reflex curled my arm to my breast. Upon examination, I determined that a blister would soon form from the burn on my index hand. I looked up to find the woman clucking to the creature and stroking the top of its head.

"Are you daft, man? That is most certainly not the way to approach a dragon."

How dare she scold me! And yet the throbbing of my burnt finger tempered my response. "Well, madame, what *is* the proper protocol to approach a dragon?"

She reached underneath her table and retrieved a tin box, scarcely larger than a deck of playing cards. Using small metal tongs, she picked up a tidbit of a dark and glossy substance.

"Here." She handed me the instrument and its cargo. "Move slowly and feed Kék Láng—" she raised the blue dragon slightly— "the liver."

With much trepidation, I did as she asked, and the dragonlet made a growling purr as she devoured the meat. Her brother, unable to escape the crate, clamored for his own reward.

The woman held out the box and tilted her head to the restless black dragon. "Go ahead. Give Szakadék a morsel."

I clasped a dark red lump with the tiny tongs and lowered it toward the black dragon. Szakadék hopped and flapped his wings, nearly knocking the tongs from my hand on several occasions before he gobbled his own treat.

He was such a comical fellow, I could not help but chuckle. "Your price, madame?"

"Two pounds. Each."

"That's very dear."

She shrugged. "That is the price. If you cannot afford it…"

Four pounds! Of course, I could afford four pounds. "I shall have them both." I retrieved a five-pound note from my wallet. "I require no change."

She handed me a pamphlet. "I've had a brochure printed regarding proper care and feeding of young dragons, and I highly recommend you follow it to the letter."

It simply would not do to keep dragons in my Belgrave Square townhome. I covered the crate with a woolen blanket and brought it to my country house, with Simmons—my coachman—none the wiser, as I had an array of holiday packages.

We arrived late in the evening, and I did not wish to wake Mrs. Hightower, so I had my butler bring me the remains of a mutton and kidney pie from the kitchen. The two dragons made short work of it and fell fast asleep with rounded bellies. But that left me one matter of concern.

I pulled out the brochure and skimmed through its contents until I found the necessary topic. According to the paper, the dragonlets would be contented with a shallow tray of earth for their privy. I slipped out of my room and crept down the stairs to the kitchen. The candle was half burnt down by the time I located one of Mrs. Hightower's baking pans. Ashe had been putting in some new rose beds, you see, so I knew I should find plenty of loose dirt there. I made my way outside, filled the pan, and padded back upstairs without waking anyone.

I set the soil near the sleeping lizards and washed my hands in the basin. Typically, I would have already arisen before Greenwood came to wake me in the morning, so I had no fear of him stumbling upon the reptiles.

As I prepared for bed, I debated whether or not to return Kék Láng and Szakadék to their crate, but decided against it, in the event I awakened them. I craved nothing more than my own deep repose, and sooner rather than later.

Even so, I felt I should prepare myself for the morrow. I sat at my desk to read through the brochure with more care. My eyelids weighed heavy as I sat in my most comfortable armchair. On the third page, there was a blot of ink that I had not recalled from my previous inspection. It transfixed my gaze, and as I gawped at the paper, it seemed not to be a blot of ink, but a hole.

A faint noise issued from it, as of metal scraping upon stone. I stared, perplexed, as the sound got louder. After a moment, light glinted off something moving inside the aperture. Lamplight reflected off glossy skin as its frenzied movements brought it closer and closer to the top of the cleft. I could not see the thing clearly, but it seemed to my mind to be a great spider, though smooth and scaled rather than hairy.

My breath came fast and shallow, and yet I could neither move nor tear my eyes from the scrambling horror.

"I am coming," a gravelly voice whispered in my ear.

With a gasp, I jerked away from the table. The pamphlet lay as before, unmarked and unblemished. It was nothing more than a dream. I surrendered to my weariness and retired for the night.

"Good morning, sir."

Greenwood stood next to my bed.

"Good day to you." I yawned and stretched. Some small thing at the back of my brain seemed unreasonably alarmed that I had overslept. "What are my appointments today?"

"Sir, you are having tea with Lady Hemsworth, then attending Christmas Eve at your sister's house. Also, the builders are scheduled to arrive at ten this morning to repair the stable roof."

"Yes. Thank you, Greenwood."

A flash of blue caught my eye as it disappeared out the open door. *The dragons!*

"Yes, yes. Very good. I'll be down for breakfast in a moment." I hurried my butler out the door.

I looked inside the crate, on the remote possibility that Szakadék had not joined his sister in her mad rush out of my chamber. Alas, he must have led the charge. I did note that at least one of them had taken advantage of the earth tray.

I dressed as hurriedly as possible and fairly trotted out of my bedroom. It would not do to alert the staff, of course. I searched each room with an open door, and for all my trouble, found naught but a blue dragon scale the size of my ring fingernail in the corridor. I plucked it up and slipped it into my trouser pocket.

On the pretext of taking in a brisk morning walk, I surveyed the grounds and perused the outbuildings. I had spent the better part of two hours in such pursuits when I came upon Simmons and Ashe embroiled in conversation near the coach house. I hid myself around the corner so I could listen to them unawares.

Ashe: "… blasted badgers! The varmints have been rooting about in the new rose beds."

I would have chuckled had I not been eavesdropping! It would do him no good to know that I, in fact, was the 'badger.'

Simmons: "Perhaps they've made away with the stable boy. I can't find that lazy lump anywhere."

That gave me pause. Surely the missing dragons and missing stable boy were in no way related. I reckoned the dragons were but small, but they were dragons, nonetheless.

I continued my perambulation of the property. The builders had arrived and were engaged in their task of roof repair. It occurred to me that the rooftop should be a most excellent vantage point for my endeavor.

"Good morning. Are you the head man?"

The workman took off his cap. "No, sir. He's up there." He jerked his thumb upward.

"I see. Do be a good chap and secure the ladder whilst I climb up and have a word."

"Yes, sir!" He scurried over and gripped the rails as I clambered up. Three men worked at replacing broken tiles. A fourth leaned against the cupola.

I approached the leaning man. "Good morning! I take it you're the head man?"

"That I am."

"The repairs look very... well done." I scanned the grounds from my perch. *Oh, dear.* One of Mrs. Hightower's chickens was running through the kitchen garden, wings a-flap. I caught glimpses of blue and black amongst the rosemary. "Yes, thank you. Carry on!"

I skittered down the ladder and rushed to the battleground.

By the time I arrived, the reptilian miscreants had cornered the poor hen between the Brussels sprouts and the leeks. I was closest to Szakadék, so I tip-toed up behind him and snatched him up. Oh, the hissing and screeching! His teeth missed my hand by scarcely a hair's breadth. And yet I folded his wings and tucked him into my waistcoat. Perhaps it was a failing of memory, but he seemed to have grown to half again the size he was last night.

Her brother's energetic protestations distracted Kék Láng from her hunt. She flapped her wings and took to the air. I leaped to grab her and caught the end of her tail, nearly landing upon the disgruntled chicken.

I tucked Kék Láng in next to her brother, and the two of them almost popped the buttons off my waistcoat, so tight was the fit and so much did they wriggle and writhe. I buttoned my overcoat and kept my arm across my abdomen, to prevent the dragonlets from tumbling out.

As I made for the staircase, Greenwood intercepted me. "Ah, there you are, sir. Mrs. Hightower is ready for luncheon to be served. As you skipped your breakfast, she is fretting about your good health."

I detected a wrinkle in his brow as his eyes fell on my squirming midsection. "My health is excellent! Inform Mrs. Hightower that I shall be down for lunch in short order."

He turned toward the kitchen, and I made my way up the stairs, with as much dignity as I could muster under the circumstances. I shut the dragons in their crate—despite their chattering—and went to my repast.

I ate a few morsels, then I said to Greenwood, "I have many administrative tasks to complete ere I leave to have tea with Lady Hemsworth. I shall finish my meal in my chambers."

And I will tell you I did not care what he thought of me when I added a second pork chop to my plate before climbing the stairs.

I liberated the two lizards from their box so they may partake of their supper. They gobbled the meat—one pork chop each—greedily. After their messy meal, they groomed each other as cats are wont to do, then curled up to sleep. This time I shut them in the crate before I left for my appointment.

When I returned from Lady Hemsworth's tea, it was nearly full dark. Forgetting myself as I disembarked, I asked of Simmons, "Did you locate your errant stable boy?"

He gave me the queerest of looks. "Yes, sir. Mrs. Hightower had sent him to fetch some apples from the Drably estate, sir."

"Ah! All's well that ends well, I suppose."

"Yes, sir."

The bottom floor of the house was brightly lit as Simmons went to change out the horses. I proceeded up to my chambers to check on the dragonlets. I had yet to work out how I would get their crate down the stairs and into the carriage, with the contents remaining undetected.

The lamps in my bedchamber were unlit. Greenwood had never failed in the task before, so unease settled over me. The baby dragons were restless in their confinement, growling and chirping as they paced from end to end.

Wind stirred the silhouettes of trees in the dark and they whipped back and forth in a frenzy. The dragonlets became more animated.

A massive shadow blotted out the sky. It slid down the window for what felt to be a very long time. When it stopped, glowing yellow eyes the size of dinner plates glared through the glass.

"I am here," the same gravelly voice from last night whispered. It seemed to come from inside my head, rather than from the creature.

The shadow was blacker than the surrounding sky. I could make out the form of a massive dragon. I glanced over my shoulder at the young ones. "Is this your mother?"

They clamored in the crate, desperate to get out. I picked up the box and carried it to the window. When I opened the glass, hot, sulfurous breath raked my skin.

"Here, ma'am. Here you go." I opened the box and took first Kék Láng and then Szakadék and set them on the windowsill.

The huge dragon outstretched her nose, and the two clambered on and settled behind the great spikes on her head. Her prodigious wings flapped, and she rose into the night sky.

"And that, my dear nephew, is why you're getting a pair of bright sovereigns for Christmas."

Reginald's eyes were wide as he reached out his hand to take the gold coins.

"Thank you, Uncle Payton!" Reginald stuffed the two sovereigns into his sock. Then he swept up his new hobby horse and galloped off toward the conservatory.

My sister crossed her arms. "It seems you have availed yourself of that copy of *The Arabian Nights Entertainments* I gave you for your birthday. You're a veritable Scheherazade."

"Perhaps, my dear Emma. Perhaps."

"Next time, you needn't resort to such flights of fancy. Just advise me prior to the event and I shall get him a proper gift, with your name upon it. Cash money is thoughtless and vulgar.

Although… I should have liked to have a small dog around the house. Pity there were no pups to be had."

I smiled and nodded, fingering the turquoise blue dragon scale in my pocket.

THE RED SCARF
By A. B. Richards

DULL morning light filtered in through the kitchen window. I did a double take as I rinsed my coffee mug. *Who in the world built a snowman out there?* I have no close neighbors, and my children are adults living in far-flung cities.

The candy-apple-red scarf and a not-quite matching red hat were bright pops of color against the overcast sky. It was a little too distant to make out the details of its face, but the carrot nose pointed toward the street.

Wait. Gabe has a scarf like that. I smiled out the window. I hadn't felt well yesterday afternoon after an afib episode, and I'd missed going with him to the Christmas cantata. A prescription sleeping pill, a dose of metoprolol, and ten hours of sleep had put me to rights.

Gabe must have come during the night and built the snowman to cheer me up. That was exactly the sort of thing he'd do. I called Gabe to thank him for the surprise snowman, but it rolled to voice mail. *Probably in the bathroom or something.*

I scowled at the dirty plate and silverware in the sink, certain I'd cleaned up the kitchen last night. It was like one of those creepy stories where a family thinks their house is haunted, but it turns out there's a homeless person squatting in their attic. I was up there two days ago to fetch the Christmas decorations, and there was no sign of vagrants. I loaded the dishes into the dishwasher and made my way to the living room.

My three kids and their families would blow into town throughout the next week, and I knew I'd better finish my decorating before the toddlers arrived and wanted to 'help.' I love my grandkids more than life, but some of my holiday items are fragile family heirlooms best kept from their not-so-tender ministrations. They could help me bake cookies—flour's easy to clean up.

I put my hands on my hips. "Where is that damn water bottle?"

Tangelo, my extra fluffy orange cat, snapped his head up and pricked his ears toward the kitchen, staring intently ahead. Then he scrambled off the couch and slunk down the hall to hide in my bedroom. He only did that when someone was at the door.

"What's gotten into you?" I walked over to the entryway and peered through the peephole. I saw nothing, so I stepped out onto the frosty stoop to see if anyone was coming up the lane. No sidewalks this far out of town.

The frozen Sunday morning was undisturbed. Except…

I thought the snowman was farther away from that tree? I slammed the door and locked it.

The ugly voice that sometimes popped up in my head chuckled. *Getting a little forgetful?*

I slapped my hand on the wall. *Of course it hasn't moved! Just the difference in perspective from looking at it from the kitchen window versus the front porch, that's all.*

I turned to my right and walked through my tiny formal living room into the small dining room—which I'd repurposed into a study—and made another right into the kitchen.

My water bottle was exactly where I had left it—on the counter by the sink. That was expected, but the shimmering colored lights on the Christmas tree in the den were not. *I don't remember turning them on. Perhaps I'm so distracted by that weird snowman that I can't keep track of what I'm doing.*

Maybe you're losing your mind. You are *getting long in the tooth,* the ugly little voice sneered.

I shuddered. *Shut up! I'm not listening to you.*

I called Gabe again. This time I left a voice mail.

At two miles to the northwest, he and his brother, Jasper, are my closest neighbors—unless you counted the livestock that was pastured on three sides of me and across the road. The brothers are partially off the grid, so they spend much of their day outside chopping wood and that sort of thing. At this point, I wasn't too worried.

The knock at the front door made me jump. I hurried to see who it was. Two bundled-up young women I didn't recognize stood on my front porch. One carried a folder.

"Can I help you with something?" I called from behind the door. No way I was opening it.

"Yes, ma'am," said the lady with the folder. "Do you have a minute? We'd like to share the Good News with you."

"Good news? Did you win the lottery and you're passing out cash? That's the kind of good news I want to hear."

"No, sorry. But our news is even better!" chirped the second woman.

"I don't care for a sermon, thanks. Have a nice day."

"But we're here to save you from eternal torment!" whined the folder girl.

I planned to ignore her, but changed my mind. "I would recommend that you two be careful wandering around out here. Mavis Hardesty went missing last week without a trace. You never know what kind of crazy people are going to drift into the area—there's a rail line that runs through town. I still want you to leave my property, though."

The pair looked at each other for a long moment, then shuffled down the walkway to where their car was parked on the road.

"Okay, Tangelo. You can come out now." He was already winding around my legs and purring.

I scooped him up and sat on the couch with him in my lap, scratching the top of his head. *No updates on Mavis. She was always a little flakey, but I can't imagine she'd just leave town without a word to anyone. Hope she's okay wherever she is.*

Tangelo squirmed out of my arms and started making biscuits on the knitted afghan that lay crumpled on one of the cushions. "I see how you are. I need to finish my decorating, anyway."

By early afternoon, I had all the breakables safely out of reach from sticky little hands. *It looks very Christmasy, if I do say so myself.* The kitchen and large den are connected by an open counter, a few inches higher than the cooktop. I could easily admire my freshly trimmed tree as I made lunch.

The text chime on my phone sounded. It was a message from Jasper. "Can you send my lay-about brother home? Firewood won't split itself."

My stomach clenched, and I swallowed hard before I called him.

He answered before the first ring. "Hey, Miriam. I hate to interrupt a good time, but there's some weather coming in later, and we've got to get those logs split and stacked."

"Gabe isn't here."

Moments of silence followed. "What do you mean, he's not there? He was going to stop by your place to check on you on the way back from the cantata. I just assumed he'd spent the night."

"I never saw him."

Jasper muttered a string of swear words. "Let's go find him. Be there in five." He disconnected.

Now I'm officially worried. I hurriedly put on my boots, coat, and hat. I reached into my pocket for gloves and pulled out a carrot. It took a moment to remember the horses from across the road were up by the fence yesterday.

I was locking up when Jasper's silver truck skidded to a stop in front of the garage. He got out and stood frowning before closing the door. "Your grandkids here already?"

"No. Why? Oh… I don't know where that snowman came from. It was there when I woke up this morning. I thought perhaps Gabe had…."

"Looks like his scarf." Jasper's Adam's apple bobbed. "Do you think Mavis' disappearance is in any way related to Gabe's?" He motioned for me to follow him as he started toward the snowman.

"No idea. I mean, I assumed t it was just Mavis being Mavis, but now that Gabe is missing, too…."

We walked down the driveway to the cleared road, instead of adventuring through the wet snow—it was only about five or six inches deep, but the ground underneath was uneven. The snowman was probably 40 or 50 yards from my house.

He cheerfully perched in his red ensemble in front of the fence. There was a three-foot gap between the wood and the edge of the ditch, and the bottom ball of the snowman took up the entire margin. There were some indentations, especially in the ditch, that were probably footprints leading from the snowman to the road, but it appeared that precipitation had dropped after they were made. The white layer near the snowman was noticeably thinner where it had been gathered to build the icy sculpture before a fresh dusting had fallen.

I lifted one end of the red scarf and a pile of accumulated snow fluttered to the ground. "That is definitely the scarf I knitted Gabe for Christmas last year." I noticed there was a hole in it, as if it had gotten caught on something and broken some of the yarn.

The hat was the generic sort found at any discount store. I wasn't sure if that's why it seemed familiar, or if it was because someone I knew had one like it.

A gust of wind puffed loose snow across the pavement, its icy needles stinging my cheek.

Jasper zipped his coat. "I agree. Let's get back to my truck and head towards town. *His* truck has to be somewhere."

We hurried towards my house, and I was glad to get inside the warm vehicle. Our search didn't take long. The road sloped down and curved about a mile and a half from my place. Gabe's red truck was part-way on the shoulder, with the hood up and the flashers going.

I jumped out of Jasper's vehicle before it had completely stopped, stumbling as I ran. "Gabe! Gabe, are you here?"

Jasper tried the door. It was locked, and the keys were gone. Fresh snow blanketed the bed of the truck, but there was none under the hood. The engine must have still been warm when the snow fell.

"Shit," Jasper spat. "I'm calling 9-1-1. Stand over here with me and don't touch anything."

Deputy Casey Bower arrived about ten minutes after the call.

"That was quick." Jasper pulled his hat down against the fresh breeze.

"Yeah, well, I was just down the road. Mavis Hardesty's daughter went to get a roast out of the deep freeze and found poor old Mavis in there."

I gasped. "How awful! Who would do such a terrible thing?"

"Well, ma'am, I can't really talk about an ongoing investigation. But it could have been an accident. You know Mavis was five foot nothing and probably didn't weigh ninety pounds soaking wet. Her daughter said she always stood on a stepstool to reach down into the freezer. She could have lost her balance and fallen in."

That's a lot of talking, for something you're not supposed to be talking about. "She had the book club meeting at her house the night before she disappeared. She was perfectly fine then." *How could she be dead?*

"Yes, ma'am. I will need to talk to you about that. Would you mind sitting in Jasper's truck? Jasper, have a seat in my car. You can sit in the front. I'm gonna have a look around Gabe's truck, and then I'll take your statements. The regional forensics team is at Mavis' house, and they'll come by here when they're done."

Jasper tossed me his keys and got into Deputy Bower's car. I climbed into Jasper's truck, started the engine, and set the heater on high. By the time the deputy finished his inspection, I had gone from shivering to sweating. I turned down the heat, but still had to open the window for a minute to let out some of the hot air. There was a little flipping in my chest, as if a tiny bird was trapped under my collarbone. I checked my watch. My heart rate was elevated, but nothing crazy. Which was good, because my medicine was back at the house.

Another cruiser arrived, lights flashing, and that deputy had a word with Bower before coming over to Jasper's truck, laptop in hand. The wind tossed the long copper braid that hung down her back.

She opened the passenger door and sat down. "Afternoon, Ms. Vickery. I'm Deputy Morgenstern. I'll be taking your statements." She opened the computer and started typing and adjusting the angle of the lid. After a minute or two, she looked at me. "I'm advising you that this interview is being video recorded, and a transcript will be made available to you. Okay. Let's start with Mr. Martinez. When was the last time you saw him?"

"Well… we were supposed to go to the cantata last night, but I was ill—I have a heart condition—and I just took my heart medication and a sleeping pill and turned in early. The day before, I caught a ride into town with him. He dropped me at the post office, then ran to the feed store. We met at Mabel's and got a bite to eat, and he brought me back home. So, last time I saw him was Friday lunch."

"And what brought you out here today?"

"Jasper called and told me to send Gabe home, but he wasn't at my house. He said that Gabe had planned to stop by last night, but if he did, it was after I took my sleeping pill, and I wouldn't have known anything about it. Jasper picked me up, and we found Gabe's truck."

"Did Mr. Martinez often spend the night at your home?"

I knew this was coming. "It depends. Sometimes twice a week, but a month or more might go by before he stayed over."

"So, you were romantically involved with Gabe Martinez?"

I sighed. *It's complicated.* "Yes and no. I mean, we did have… relations. I'm not denying that. But my husband passed away ten years ago, and his wife left him… I think it's been three or four years now. We've always been good friends—known each other since grade school. And sometimes a body needs some human comfort. But we're not dating or anything like that."

"I understand."

Do you? "There's something else. When I woke up this morning, there was a snowman, wearing the scarf I'd made for Gabe, a little ways down from my house."

"Are there kids in the area? Was there anything unusual about it?"

"No kids within a few miles. When Jasper arrived, we checked it out. It was only a snowman. With Gabe's scarf. And a hat. I'm not sure where that came from. It doesn't quite match."

"Interesting. We'll have forensics take a look. How would you describe the relationship between Jasper and Gabe?"

"Well, they're brothers. They get along well enough, as far as I know. Jasper took him in after his divorce. They have disagreements, sure, but I've never seen anything heated between them."

Deputy Morgenstern nodded, as if what I'd told her was common knowledge. I supposed it was, for anybody who'd lived in the area for more than a month.

"Ms. Vickery? Do you have any idea why there's blood on the grill guard of Jasper's truck?"

"I'm sorry? What?"

"There's dried blood on the heavy-duty bars over the grill of Jasper's truck. I was wondering if he'd mentioned anything about it to you."

I felt like she'd slapped me across the face. "No. No, he didn't say anything to me about any blood."

"Okay, thank you for that. I'm going to end this interview, and then we'll talk about Mavis Hardesty."

I was still reeling from that ambush question. Jasper would never hurt Gabe. I don't think. I wracked my brain. Had there been red yarn fibers anywhere on the push bars? I didn't remember any, but I hadn't paid attention, either.

"Alright, Ms. Vickery. I'm ready to start the second interview. Again, it is being recorded and there will be a transcript."

"Sure. Where should I start?"

"How about the book club meeting?"

"There were five of us. Mavis, of course. Me. Jenny Silver, Elizabeth Farrow, and Fatima Sidiqi. We talked about the book. I hate the main character... Jenny wants to be her. Mavis had put out some little snacks for us. Something must have had MSG in it because all around my mouth started feeling numb and I got a splitting headache. It triggered my afib—always does—so I took one of my pills, and when my heartbeat was stable, I left. I drank a ton of water to try to flush my system. But I had such a bad headache I had to take a sleeping pill to get any rest."

"And what are these medications?"

"Hold on." I opened the pharmacy app on my phone and pulled up my last order, then held the screen up to the webcam on the deputy's laptop.

"And you take the metoprolol daily?"

"I'm supposed to. But I'm too young for Medicare, and my bargain-basement insurance fights me on every prescription. So, I just take it when I have an attack."

"And the sleeping pill?"

"Only when I need it. It knocks me out—a bomb could go off and I wouldn't know it. I mean, I may as well be a corpse."

"Okay. Thank you. Back to the book club meeting. Before you left, were there any altercations? Did anyone seem agitated or upset in any way?"

"Other than me, with my MSG reaction? No." An image popped up in my mind. "Now that you mention it, Lizzie seemed to be in a bad mood. But she never said why."

"That's Elizabeth Farrow?"

"Yes."

About that time, the doors of Deputy Bower's car opened, and both men stepped out. The deputy walked around and handcuffed Jasper.

"What's he doing?" I shouted as Bower put my friend in the back of his car.

"He's going back to HQ for a more in-depth interview. Handcuffs are protocol. It's nothing personal. I'll give you a lift back to your place and you can show me the snowman. Turn off the engine and hand me the keys."

"What if Gabe is out in the snow somewhere, hurt? I've gotta keep looking for him!"

"Ms. Vickery. It appears that his truck broke down. He either started walking toward your house or back into town. Your house is closer. If you and his brother didn't find him alongside the road, I don't think that's the case. But there is a bloodhound on the way, should arrive within the hour."

I leaned on the kitchen sink and stared out the window. The forensics team had seemed to be in no hurry coming from Mavis' house. They'd spent about ten minutes taking photos of the snowman. I don't know what else I expected them to do. Snow had started falling again. Not heavy, yet, but it wouldn't be long. The black and white Crime Scene Investigation Team van stood out, along with the red scarf waving in the wind. The hat had blown off some time ago, and I had no idea where it was. Looked like they were packing up to leave. One of them brought out a paper bag and stuffed the scarf inside.

The world had become surreal. Gabe, missing. Jasper, detained by the police with blood on his truck. *There had to be another explanation. Jasper would never hurt Gabe. There was still a chance he was alive somewhere. No body had been found.* I exhaled loudly. *Yet.*

The ugly little voice snickered. *If he's been lying around injured somewhere all this time, in this weather, he's most certainly a corpse-cicle.*

I ignored it and called Gabe again. Every single investigator turned toward the snowman. I swallowed the bile that rose in my throat. *No.*

One person retrieved the camera and set it up on a tripod.

Gabe's phone rolled to voice mail.

The rest of the team crossed the ditch.

No. I disconnected and set the phone down.

They began brushing the snowman. Chunks of snow collapsed to the ground as they carefully broke apart the top. Something dark was under the snow.

Hair.

Flesh.

Collar of a flannel shirt.

Gabe.

No! I covered my face with my hands and sobbed. After I caught my breath, I splashed water on my face and blotted it dry.

Told you so. The ugly voice seemed more smug than usual.

Shut up! Shut up! Shut up!

I didn't want to look out the window, but I couldn't help myself. I wish I had more self-control. They'd uncovered most of Gabe, and even from this distance, I could see how bloody he was. How his arm was bent in too many places. He had been my friend, and I loved him. It killed me to see him like that. I fled to the back bedroom and flung myself on the bed.

Surely it was an accident. Gabe's truck broke down, and he was walking to my house. Jasper must have had some late errand, didn't see Gabe in the dark, and hit him. That explains the blood on the truck and Gabe's mangled body. But why the snowman? And why not stop to help his own brother? Both the snowman and the hit-and-run seemed completely out of character for Jasper. Had they had a fight that had so enraged him that he'd murder his own brother? *No. I just couldn't believe it.*

A shadow moved across the wall. Tangelo hopped up on the bed and started kneading my stomach. I reached up to stroke him, and my finger caught in a collar, mostly buried in his long hair. *When did I buy that?*

The ugly little voice sounded so smug. *Must be brain rot. I could tell you, but you're always yelling at me to shut up.*

I keep all my receipts to reconcile my bank account. Surely, I'd find a clue there. I retrieved my wallet and began thumbing through the contents. Gas receipt, grocery receipt. Expired coupon. A twenty-dollar bill.

A Walmart receipt.

At 2:17 AM, today. *What?*

I scanned down the list of purchased items. A green cat collar. Box of frozen blueberry waffles. Men's deodorant. Pack of ballpoint pens. *Why? I didn't need any of those things.*

No. No, I was asleep. Dead to the world. *Is someone trying to gaslight me? Who? Why?* When I took one of those sleeping pills, a brass band could march around my house playing the *1812 Overture* and I would never know. It would be a simple thing for anyone to plant the receipt and leave dishes in the sink to make me think I was losing my mind. *But who would do that? Who has a key?*

Jasper and Gabe.

Mavis.

She looks after Tangelo when I go to visit my grandkids. My address is messed up in the GPS system. Delivery drivers can never find my place, so I often have packages delivered to Mavis' house.

To which I have a key.

My insides froze. *That red hat from the snowman. Mavis had one just like it. Am I next? Is the person who put Mavis in the deep freeze coming for me?* I took the collar off Tangelo and threw it toward the trash can.

I had to call Deputy Morgenstern. My phone was in the kitchen, so I got up to retrieve it. It started ringing before I even got to the den. I jogged to answer it. Jasper's name flashed across the screen.

"Are you home?"

"Yeah. They had nothing to hold me on. I hit a deer a couple of days ago, that's why I had blood on my truck. But they had to do some test to show it wasn't human blood. Are you okay? I guess you know they found Gabe." His voice broke.

"I *saw* them find him." Couldn't say more without breaking down.

"I was afraid of that."

"Look, I'm glad you're home. Really, I am. But can I call you back in a few? It's kind of urgent."

"Sure. Talk soon."

I got her card out and punched in Morgenstern's number. Her voice sounded tired. "Deputy Mor—"

"I need your help. I think someone's planning to kill me."

"What? Ms. Vickery, is that you?"

I told her all about the Mavis key and hat situation.

31

"Let me get this straight. You have a key to Mavis Hardesty's house? That answers a lot of questions."

"Yes. And she has a key to mine. I told you that. What are you going to do to keep me from ending up like her?"

"Well, Ms. Vickery, why don't you come on into my office and we can talk about it? I was just about to call you, anyway."

"Why?"

"Security camera footage has been uploaded from Mavis' neighborhood. Feel free to bring an attorney with you."

"I didn't do anything. I don't need a lawyer." And I most certainly did not want to be here in my house alone. "Is now good? Can I come in now?"

"Of course. Drive carefully."

"I'm headed to my car."

Hopefully, she'll put me in protective custody. Cooling my heels in jail would be a lot better than being shoved into my own deep freeze. And I'd be released as soon as they found the killer. How bad can the slammer be for a couple of days?

On the way to the garage, I called Jasper and asked him to feed Tangelo, in case I was away for a while. He seemed very concerned, but I told him everything would be fine. Especially after they caught the murderer.

I clicked the button and snow blew in. A snowstorm's not the best time to drive, but if I took it slowly, it would be all right. And it sure beat being snowbound with a killer on the loose.

The driver's side mirror dangled by a few wires. *What the heck?*

I walked around to the front of the compact SUV. My head went woozy, and nausea clenched my stomach.

The hood had a human-sized dent in it. A bloody spiderweb glittered across most of the windshield.

And caught in the grill was a tuft of red yarn fibers.

The ugly little voice in my head laughed.

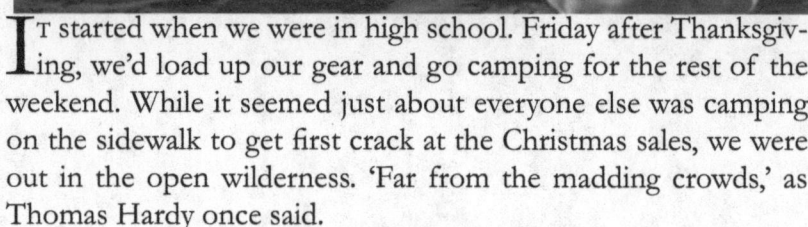

BlackFriday
By A. B. Richards

IT started when we were in high school. Friday after Thanksgiving, we'd load up our gear and go camping for the rest of the weekend. While it seemed just about everyone else was camping on the sidewalk to get first crack at the Christmas sales, we were out in the open wilderness. 'Far from the madding crowds,' as Thomas Hardy once said.

Okay. Perhaps 'wilderness' is going a bit far. We'd pick a state park or national forest within a couple hours' drive so that we were away from civilization, but not *too* far away. Max and Toby were married now, and Max has two kids. Ben was thinking about proposing to his girlfriend on Christmas Eve. Me, I hadn't come across the right person yet. And truth be told, I haven't exactly been looking.

"Afternoon. You camping?" The park ranger poised a pen over his clipboard.

"Yes. We have a reservation. Under Sloane Scarsdale."

He stepped inside and returned with a map and a parking permit. "Stick this inside your windshield on the driver's side." He gave me a receipt with tape on the ends, then opened the map. "Here's your campsite, highlighted in yellow."

"Got it. Thanks."

He raised his hand in dismissal as I rolled up the window. I handed the map over to Toby, who slouched in the passenger seat. "Okay. Navigate us."

Toby took it and sucked his teeth. "You think we'll see it?"

"See what?" Ben asked from the back seat.

"The Swamp Thing."

Ben and Max chuckled.

"Goin' on a bigfoot hunt, Toby?" Max leaned forward.

Toby shrugged. "People say they've seen something. Not my place to say they haven't."

"Turn left or stay straight?" I knew where to go. I just wanted to break off this conversation. Ben and Max sometimes took things too far, and Toby usually got the worst of it.

"Um…" Toby stared at the map. "Straight."

The campsites were arranged in a wide oval. Ours was at the end closer to the trails. Only one other pad was taken, and it was at the end closer to the road.

We set up our tents and started cooking on Max's camp stove. I don't know how we went wrong with the potatoes, but they took much longer than anticipated. That meant our after-supper hike began at twilight. Which was probably okay. The moon was nearly full, and the trails were pretty well maintained. It didn't hurt that the trailhead was next to our campsite. It made a loop a little over a mile long, down to the river and back.

Ben and I sat on a log, listening to the sounds of the river and the night creatures. Max and Toby stood near the riverbank, watching a raccoon dig for mussels. I may not have my Christmas shopping done, but I feel stress dropping off me like a dirty cloak.

Ben yawned. "I'm ready to go." He stretched his legs out before standing.

"Me, too." Toby turned away from the river.

I got to my feet. Between the long drive, setting up camp and cooking, and the fresh night air, I was drowsy as well.

We hadn't gone more than thirty yards down the trail when Max stopped. "What's that?"

All of us pivoted in the direction he pointed. Something light-colored crawled between the trees. It was too far away to see it clearly, but my brain started sounding alarm bells.

Ben scoffed. "Probably a coyote."

"No." Max said. "It's far too big. We should keep moving and get out of its territory."

We all looked at each other, faces unreadable in the dark. When I glanced at the creature, it was a lot closer than it had been a moment before. It began to lope toward us on over-long limbs.

"Run!" I took off at a sprint, not looking to see who was following. I heard footsteps pounding along in my wake.

I was the first to make it to the tents. Max was seconds behind me. Toby arrived a minute later.

"Where's Ben?" I panted.

Toby leaned over, his hands on his thighs. "Thought I was the last."

"Shit!" Max, who ran marathons and hadn't even broken a sweat, paced around the fire ring. "We can't leave him out there."

"Agreed." I tried to tamp down my sense of existential dread.

Dry leaves crunched and crackled. Ben strolled into the campsite. "Why were you so afraid? It was nothing, just a loose dog."

That thing didn't look like any dog I'd ever seen. But I was tired, and it was dark, so maybe my eyes were playing tricks. "Discretion is the better part of valor."

"Makes sense." Toby unzipped his tent. "The Swamp Thing is more of a bigfoot type creature, anyway."

Ordinarily, we would sit around the campfire and talk, some-times into the wee hours. But fall had been unusually dry and warm, so there was a fire ban in the park. May as well call it a night.

"See you in the morning." I opened my own tent.

"Night." Max headed toward the restrooms.

I was the second one up. Max already had coffee on the boil and was cracking eggs into a large bowl.

He started whisking the liquid. "Morning!"

How is anybody this cheerful at this time of day? "Hey, Max." I raised the plastic bag with my toothbrush and continued on my way to the bathrooms.

I passed Toby on my way back. Ben sat in a canvas camp chair near the table Max had set up for the stove. It was a little odd that he was in Toby's seat, but I don't suppose it really mattered. I put my toiletries away and pulled out my own chair.

Max stirred the potato cubes and bacon in the skillet. "So, where did it come from?"

Ben looked at me and back at Max. "Where did what come from?"

"The loose dog."

"Oh. The dog. From the other campsite."

"Where the RVs are?" I asked.

"RVs. Yes." Ben nodded slowly.

Max chuckled. "Dude must be in sticker shock over that ring."

I laughed and Ben smiled awkwardly, his mouth open.

I reacted to the stench without thinking. "Ben. Seriously. Go brush your teeth."

Max poured the beaten eggs over the potatoes and continued stirring. Ben got up and ambled to his tent, emerging moments later with a zippered bag. Saying nothing, he started on the trek to the bathrooms.

When I thought he was out of earshot, I turned to Max. "Do you think he's okay? His breath smells like something dead."

"Lotta people have dragon breath first thing in the morning."

"You talking about me?" Toby returned, a damp washcloth slung over his shoulder.

"Ben seems a bit distracted." Max took a small sample of his egg concoction and tasted it, then proceeded to add more seasonings.

Toby flopped into his chair, putting his toiletry bag in the cupholder. "Probably thinking about his proposal and considering the death of his bachelorhood."

"Yeah. I was at his place a couple of days ago, and he showed me the ring. He's pretty nervous about popping the question to Gwen."

"He shouldn't be." Max dug a package of tortillas out of a plastic bin. "She's all but proposed to him. Not like she's gonna turn him down."

I got up, poured myself a cup of coffee, and sifted in several tablespoons of powdered creamer.

"Breakfast is served." Max made a sweeping gesture across the camp stove.

I put my coffee in the cupholder of my chair and moved into line behind Toby to serve myself some breakfast.

Ben returned, raised his head, and inhaled deeply. "That smells like food."

"Um… Thanks?" Max dropped a couple of flour tortillas onto his plate.

"You are welcome." Ben deposited his things in his tent, then deposited his butt in my seat.

"Hey! Get your own chair, fool. You walked right past it."

Ben's eyebrows knitted. He got to his feet and retrieved the collapsed camp chair that lay by his tent. After a brief struggle with the zippered case, he unfolded the seat and sat next to Toby.

Max tilted his head. "You're not eating?"

Without a word, Ben rose and stood across the stove from Max, gazing intently as he rolled a breakfast burrito.

I swallowed what I was chewing and took a tiny sip of the very hot coffee. "I was thinking we could walk up to the oxbow lake and rent a couple of kayaks for a while, come back here and have lunch, then go out on the swamp trail."

His jaws working his breakfast, Toby nodded.

"Sounds like a plan." Max popped the last bite of burrito into his mouth.

"Yes." Ben had managed to tear the tortilla he was trying to wrap around the egg-potato-bacon mixture, which scattered over his plate.

After our leisurely breakfast, we walked across the park to the lake. They had plenty of boats, so we took our time paddling. Ben was in the kayak with me. We paused in the middle of the small lake and he leaned over and peered into the water.

"What—"

He held up a hand to shush me.

Toby and Max were coming toward us, but were probably twenty yards away.

Like an arrow, Ben's arm plunged into the water, and he pulled up a fish.

"Dude!" I laughed. "When did you learn how to do that?"

Triumphant, he raised the flopping creature aloft for the others to see.

"What are you going to do with it?" I picked up my paddle. "It'll be awhile before we get back to camp."

With a sigh, Ben lowered his prize and dropped it into the water, where it disappeared in a flash of green and silver.

"Did you see that?" I asked when Toby and Max pulled up alongside our kayak.

"Was that a fish he just reached in and grabbed?" Toby peered at Ben.

"Yeah. You're gonna have to teach us all how to do that."

I sat on the couch at Ben's house, beer in my hand and football on TV. I looked around at the clutter, which was unusual for Ben. "Busy week?"

He nodded.

My phone buzzed in my pocket. I almost ignored the text, but it had been difficult to drag words out of Ben.

Toby's name topped the message. "Where are you?"

I tapped my reply. "Ben's. Why?"

"LEAVE!!!!!"

"???"

"They found Ben's body this morning at the park. GET OUT OF THERE!"

I blinked at the screen and looked up at Ben. His arms grew longer as I gaped at him, stretching down past his knees. He folded at the hip and crawled toward me, his legs, bent and bony, protruded above his back like a spider's. As he moved, his clothes dissolved into fine grey fur.

I jumped over the couch. The monster was between me and the door, and I thought about the nightmarish speed of his arm when he caught the fish. My heart thudded against my ribs and my breath became fast and shallow.

The thing that had been pretending to be Ben opened its mouth and the reek of rotting flesh wafted over me. Uneven, needle-like teeth filled its putrid jaws.

I backed away. I could make a play for the balcony, but unless I landed in the pool, it was certain death from five floors up. The creature was blocking my path to the door. The Devil and the deep blue sea... which should I choose?

Shifting into a perfect imitation of Max's voice, it said, "Dinner is served."

Townsende and Hardwicke: Hard Core

By Artemis Greenleaf

A wooden bowl flew off a vacant table and smashed against the wall, splattering Algar Townsende and Kingsley Hardwicke with cold porridge.

"Ye gods!" Algar leapt to his feet, gruel-soaked blond hair sticking to his cheek.

Kingsley stared at his ruined beaker of cider and sighed. The simple errand the bishop had sent them upon had now become less so.

A bony monk in a threadbare cassock hurried to their table, waving a rag. "Good sirs! I pray your forbearance. We are afflicted of late by an ill-tempered spirit. Even our goodly Abbot, Father Cuthbert, has not availed in dislodging the quarrelsome sprite."

Kingsley raised an eyebrow. He would have scoffed at the very idea, had he not seen the bowl fly from the bare table of its own accord.

Algar snatched the cloth from the monk's hands and dabbed at the sticky mess clinging to his hair and cloak, muttering under his breath.

"How came you by this churlish wight, Brother Mordecai?" Kingsley pushed the tankard of porridge-sopped cider toward the monk. "There was no rumor of such ere we set upon our journey."

Mordecai cast down his eyes. "The abbot bade us hold our tongues, lest our hostelry would lay empty, and who would buy relics then? But it was the third night past Michaelmas that our persecution by this rageful ghost did begin."

Michaelmas. Was that not in the heart of November? "So you say it was near upon two months since?"

"Aye. Tomorrow is Twelfth Night. The last day of Christmas. It is scarce a week shy of two months."

Algar snorted. "Perhaps the abbot did offend some woodland shade by setting its home alight for his bonfire." He dropped the sodden rag on the table.

"Father Cuthbert eschews the feasting and merriment of Michaelmas, as it has heathen roots." Mordecai bestowed a rueful smile on his guests.

"God's body, sir! I would be naught but bones should no food pass my lips in the course of a week." Algar resumed his seat.

"It is customary to be allowed a single meal after sundown." Kingsley looked to Mordecai, who nodded.

"We shall have a modest feast upon the morrow. The abbot does not spend the church dues with abandon. While wagging tongues in the village might call him miserly, he cleaves well to the virtue of poverty."

The table began to shake. Algar and Kingsley scrambled to their feet. The monk laid his hands upon it. "In the name of the Father, the Son, and the Holy Ghost, I cast you out!"

The table redoubled its efforts.

Kingsley frowned as cider splashed from his abandoned tankard onto the table. As a veteran of King Edward's expeditions, unless it had iron that cut or teeth that bit, he had no regard for such antics. "Shall we repair to our chambers, Algar? My bones are weary, and there is much to do upon the morrow."

The abbot's glass-green eyes glittered as he looked down his aquiline nose at Kingsley, who produced from a leather pouch a batch of letters sent by the bishop. He also fetched from his pack an ornate wooden box. "As provenanced by the bishop's letters. Herein lie the hand bones of Saint Juthwara. Your abbey is well considered indeed to have not one, but two holy relics for the veneration by the faithful."

Father Cuthbert waved his hand. "There has been some interest from East Anglia with regard to Saint Ethelbert's holy dagger. But that is none of your concern."

If it were possible, his cassock was even thinner than Brother Mordecai's. He wondered whether Cuthbert's relic resale venture was ill-fated, or his tattered robe was but staging.

"I ween you are casting aspersions on our humble brotherhood. The scriptures admonish that we cannot serve both God and Mammon. The churchscot provides for our needs, so that we can feed the hungry and clothe the naked. Our reward waits in the heavenly kingdom."

Brother Mordecai burst into the abbot's offices. "Father Cuthbert! The orchard!" He paused to catch his breath.

"Well? What of it?"

"A Wyvern! The Wassail Queen scarce escaped its jaws!"

"You dalcop! A dragonet? Such a thing is naught but a fable." The abbot snorted. "A wyvern, indeed."

Algar and Kingsley's eyes met, and Kingsley cleared his throat. "As representatives of the bishop, we are obliged to investigate."

With a surprised chuckle, the abbot waved them away. "Very well, then. Go, you saddle-geese."

Half-panting, Brother Mordecai preceded them down the corridor to the hostelry, where they begeared themselves of their weapons.

"Rathe! Rathe!" the monk beseeched as they resumed their helms. "We must hurry."

He hastened ahead on the dusty road and, after some short time, they came to an orchard of apples.

Kingsley spied a single crow perched in the top of a gnarled apple tree, its glossy black head cocking to and fro as one beady coal of an eye or the other followed them.

Mordecai led them to an ancient tree, where bits of toasted bread were strewn amongst its roots.

Algar furrowed his brow. "Was this bread singed by the erstwhile wyvern?"

The monk lifted his eyes to the bare branches. "No, no. The Wassail Queen places the toast in the crown of the tree. It is to be dipped in the wassail cup and left as propitiation to the tree spirits. After an invocation, cider is poured upon the roots to bless the tree. Then the wassailing party does make a right racket to drive away any evil spirits who might have taken up residence after the harvest, and to awaken the trees."

"And the abbot condones this?" Algar glanced into the upper branches.

Mordecai rubbed his arms against the chill. "Perhaps not, but the orchard is not the province of the abbey. We make our fine cider from the apples tithed to us."

The crow flapped over to a nearby tree. Kingsley's eyes followed it. "Beseems the feisty dragonet frightened the trousers off some addlepate."

With a hand on the heft of his blade, Algar strode to the woolen pile. "God's blood!"

Kingsley and Mordecai hastened to his side.

The monk gasped, his breath rattling in his hollow chest.

"Knew you this younker?" Kingsley's glance fell upon the staring eyes of a dead man.

Mordecai made the sign of the cross. "Indeed. He is Wybert Thackere, juvenis of the lord who owns this orchard, Kenelm Thackere. Wybert had just come to the abbey as a postulant."

Kingsley frowned at the blood-soaked shirt of Wybert Thackere's mortal clay. "Misfortune has made the decision for him. Did any man begrudge him his vows?"

The monk shook his head. "No. His older brothers would inherit the lands and treasure of their father. Wybert was the youngest and sought refuge from starvation in the cloister. It is a common thing. Many prefer it over soldiering. Although it beseems his sire did pay a handsome corrody to the abbot for his care. He might never have taken vows and remained as an oblate."

Algar's lips pursed. "The wyvern must have sustained itself upon toast and had no stomach for a stripling."

"I must fetch the sheriff." Mordecai wrung his hands as he glanced up at the curious crow. "Please remain with poor Wybert to ensure no more indignities befall his corpse."

"Aye," Kingsley replied to the monk's retreating form.

Algar and Kingsley busied themselves searching for the manner of the young man's demise and any such clues as pointed to the author of his murder.

"It was no wyvern."

Both men looked up from their scrutinies to behold a maid of such surpassing beauty as to stop them in their tracks. Her raven hair uncovered, she had approached so stealthily that neither had seen nor heard her.

Kingsley regained his voice first. "Did you witness this tragedy?"

A silver ornament glittered in her hair, but her dark eyes were unreadable. "Many things I have witnessed, and I will say again this crime was not committed by a wyvern." She smoothed her green cloak.

The clop of horses' hooves on the hard-packed lane drew the attention of Kingsley and Algar.

"Perhaps Brother Mordecai is more speedy than I suspected." Kingsley craned his neck toward the road. But the small company did not slow at the orchard's entrance.

When they returned their attention to the woman, she stood there no longer.

"Suppose you that was the Wassail Queen?" Algar cast about, seeking a glimpse of the departed damsel.

"I think not. Brother Mordecai did say that she fled the wyvern with the rest of the wassailing party, after nearly being snatched by the thing. Would she return to seek it out or defend it to us?"

"Perhaps not. A fair maid from the manor?"

"If that be so, she is most fleet of foot."

Kingsley squatted on his haunches next to the slain youth. He raised one of the young man's hands and examined it and the arm.

"Look!" Algar pointed to the earth where the hand had rested moments before.

Kingsley laid the corpse's arm across its chest and picked up a silver penny. It was well worn, but otherwise ordinary.

Algar squinted at the coin. "Waylaid by brigands?"

"I do not think so." Kingsley straightened his legs. "There are no wounds on his hands or arms, as if he had raised them to defend himself against a blow or blade. Methinks his killer was known to him, and trusted, thus he did not suspect such treachery."

"A robber could have lain in wait behind the tree. The bore of it is thick enough to hide even a large carle."

"It could be as you say, but I would expect such a cowardly attack to come from behind. Poor Wybert was stabbed where his ribs open and the blade thrust up to his heart. There is little blood—his end was swift."

Algar took to searching for signs of wyvern activity, while Kingsley examined the area around the fallen postulant. Presently, they heard the galloping rhythm of horse hooves on the lane. Their pace slowed as they neared the orchard gate.

Two men, weeded as nobles, rode into the orchard.

"Ho, there!" the elder of the twain called out. "Are you the bishop's men?"

"Aye. We are Townsende and Hardwicke." Kingsley straightened his shoulders.

The younger man vaulted from his horse while it still walked and flew to the slain postulant. He clasped the still-warm body to his breast and wept.

The other dismounted his tall black horse and caught the loose mount of his companion. "I am Eadwulf Blackwoode, sheriff. He is Osgar Thackere, brother to Wybert. That reedy monk did in haste bring news of his demise. He should arrive anon with a cart to bear the boy to the abbey." Eadwulf frowned at the sobbing sibling. "Brother Mordecai did let slip the word 'wyvern,' and I fain would know what he meant."

Kingsley caught the gaze of Algar, then turned his eyes to the sheriff. "We two were in the offices of Father Cuthbert when

Brother Mordecai raced in, all a-fluster, shouting that a wyvern had accosted the wassailing party here in the orchard."

Eadwulf's eyebrow quirked. "I have not heard tell of any wyvern in these parts, not in my lifetime, nor even my grandfather's."

Algar gestured with his arm outstretched. "I have seen no sign of one, unless it has the hooves of a horse or wears leather boots upon its scalèd legs."

Kingsley discussed with the sheriff his observations on Wybert's corpse, in low tones so as not to offend the grieving Osgar. After a time, the creaking wheels of a wooden cart could be heard upon the road.

Orange torchlight flickered across the pale, blue-hued skin of Wybert Thackere as the monks washed his body and prepared him for burial. They were assisted by Osgar, while Eadwulf, Algar, and Kingsley observed the mortuary ritual.

Voices echoed off the stone corridor, more spirited than conversation but less than argument. The abbot and a well-dressed atheling strode into the chamber. Cuthbert's ragged robes looked all the poorer next to the noble's thick woolen cloak and fine clothes.

"...your Twelfth Night feast. I will not join you, nor shall my brother. My father's cooks will prepare the funerary table for the morrow. Our brother was under your care, and you have not troubled yourself for his protection. There will be no further corrody for this abbey on his behalf. Adjust your purse strings accordingly, you miserly monk."

Cuthbert's lips pressed into a thin line. Before he could respond, the noble caught sight of Eadwulf.

"Sheriff Blackwoode. It pleases me that you are already on the track of my brother's murderer. It seems you have begun a posse comitatus. Well done, my friend."

Eadwulf nodded once. "Cenric. Sorrow lies heavy upon my heart for your fallen brother. These carles are the bishop's men— Kingsley Hardwicke and Algar Townsende. As Wybert was a postulant of the abbey, they are bound to assist in apprehending his killer."

The abbot inserted himself into their conversation, his mouth puckered as if filled with sour cherries. "It is Twelfth Night. You are feasting with us, are you not?"

Eadwulf squirmed, while a hopeful mien overtook Algar's face.

"I insist upon it, Sheriff." With that, the abbot turned upon his heel and hastened away.

"Osgar. Let us quit this place. There is naught to be done for our brother, save prayers to speed his soul to rest. Our father needs the comfort of his remaining sons."

"No, Cenric. I wish to sit in vigil this evening. I shall return to the manor with tomorrow's dawn."

Cenric's nostrils flared, and his eyes flicked to the sheriff and his companions, as if his actions might have been different were there were no witnesses. "Very well then."

Osgar's eyes bore into his brother's back as he strode from the room. When he was gone, the atheling turned toward the sheriff. "Eadwulf, I do not accuse my brother of murder, but I reckon he begrudged the monies our father paid to the abbey in support of Wybert, even though Cenric stood to inherit the manor and its lands. I fear it was his belief that the corrody was the abbot picking our father's pocket. He has said more than once that, as the youngest, it was Wybert's lot to make his own way in the world."

"Did Wybert know of this?" Eadwulf stepped closer to Osgar. "Could the pair have argued?"

"I know not."

Bells tolled in the cloister belfry. Eadwulf's shoulders sagged underneath his cloak.

Kingsley cocked his head. "It does seem early for the compline."

"Not the compline. The Christmas feast." Eadwulf sighed.

"Feast?" Algar's visage brightened considerably. "Know you the way to the refectory, good sheriff?"

"Of course. But I would advise you to temper your expectations. Father Cuthbert's idea of a feast and yours may not be well-matched."

Kingsley and Algar followed Eadwulf down the dim corridors until they came to the dining hall. Monks milled about, rather than seating themselves at the long tables. The three of them jumped as a bench was violently pulled away from the table by unseen hands and overturned.

Mordecai's angry hobgoblin? Kingsley shook his head. "That does explain why they have no wish to sit. None would consent to be flung upon the stones so unceremoniously during their meal."

Algar grunted. "I am famished. *I* shall be a wrothful spirit ere long, myself!" The gurgling of his stomach punctuated his complaint.

"I heard rumor of such deviltry in the abbey but believed it the ravings of over-aled farmers." Eadwulf scanned the room.

Around them, ragged monks gobbled their repast and fled the refectory. The trio made their way to the kitchen, where they were each given a trencher and served their Christmas supper.

As they left the kitchen, Eadwulf fought to smother a smile. "I did warn you."

His face awash in dismay, Algar poked at his meager meal with his spoon, nearly knocking a flabby round of dried apple to the floor. "God's body! A bowl of leek and barley pottage? A stale crust of bread? And this…this misbegotten turnip? This is Twelfth Night feast? It is poor fare on an ordinary night."

Eadwulf chuckled. "But there is a sweet—dried fruit." He tasted his own food. "And I suspect a pork bone in the porridge."

Kingsley dodged a flying trencher that crashed against the wall. With a nod to Eadwulf, he said, "We must hasten to catch Wybert's murderer afore Algar shrivels down to bones."

Algar raised his head and inhaled deeply. "There is roast pork about!"

"Steady on." Kingsley paused to let a woman pass through a gap in the crowd. "A fine truffle pig as yourself will find the meat monger's stall in no time."

It was a market day, and the town bustled with folk, both sellers and buyers. The abbey offered no morning meal, and hunger drove the two old soldiers to the village's marketplace.

"I will find us bread, if you root out the meat." Kingsley gestured to the array of stalls ahead of them.

"Aye." Algar moved as fast as his legs would carry him amongst the crowd.

Kingsley turned and surveyed the booths arrayed to his left, which seemed as likely a direction as any. He lingered at the stall of an herb crafter, assaying the quality of their Nine Herb Charms.

"It is a buttery sprite."

"Beg pardon?" Kingsley jerked his head toward the woman's voice.

"The abbot's buttery. The sprite is angry."

She seemed oddly familiar, but he knew he had not made her acquaintance. The muted orange of her simple dress made her dark hair, threaded with grey, stand out all the more. Morning light glinted off the silver charm in her hair, and he recognized it.

Kingsley gave a little bow. "My good lady. I believe we have met your daughter."

"Oh? Whence?"

"In the apple orchard."

She smiled serenely. "Lord Thackere's orchard? There's naught but crows there this time of year."

Kingsley felt there was a secret behind her smile but could not begin to ken it. "A buttery sprite, you say?"

"Yes. Know you not of this house fae? Find the young man's killer and you shall quell its anger. The abbey will owe you double."

"Kingsley!"

He turned to see Algar waving his arms at the end of the row. Arms suspiciously empty of pork. When he turned to bid farewell to his lady acquaintance, she had gone.

With a frown, Kingsley maneuvered his way through the crowd to his colleague. "Had the meat-monger sold all his wares?"

"He had sold what few morsels he had after last night's feasting. But there are loaves aplenty, and the eel seller's stall seems well-stocked."

The pair bought enough food for the rest of the day, planning for a lack of dinner and a scant supper. And they would need to break their fasts on the morrow. They each paid for a woven wicker basket to carry their provisions back to the monastery, stopping a little near the edge of the marketplace to enjoy their cold meal.

Once their future meals were secured in their cells, they set out in search of Osgar Thackere, hoping that he'd overcome his grief enough to speak with them. They went to the chamber where Wybert's body lay, but there was not hide nor hair of Osgar.

Kingsley flagged down a passing monk. "Prithee, Brother. Would you tell us where to find Brother Mordecai?"

"He was not at lauds this morning. Father Cuthbert has sent him on some errand, I suppose. There is a grave to be dug in the churchyard, after all. And the village priest to be arranged."

Algar snorted. "I pity the poor sexton, being shaken out of his warm bed in the dead of night and sent to prick the frozen earth with his spade."

The monk bestowed them with a curt nod and hurried off to his chores.

Kingsley let out a deep breath and turned to Algar. "It might behoove us to visit the cell of Wybert Thackere. He may have left some clue behind."

"Lead the way, good sir." Algar swept his arm in front of himself, gesturing toward the dim corridor.

The pair made their way to Wybert's tiny chamber, stopping to inquire directions of more than one monk on the way. Though they searched under both his thin straw mattress and wool blanket, they found no insight into his demise. A wooden trunk at the end of his bed contained his few possessions, including two clean cassocks, but failed to yield any hint of a motive for Wybert's murder.

"Mayhap Brother Mordecai has returned from his mission." Algar scratched his chin.

"We should visit Lord Thackere's manor. It would go more smoothly if the good brother would accompany us and provide an introduction."

None of the monks they asked recalled having seen Brother Mordecai since last night's compline. After all, at 3 AM Matins, the hooded brothers could not be told apart. Finally, one suggested the Brother might be tending the chickens. They set out to find the abbey's livestock. Hens scratched at animal leavings near the stable. There were neither brothers nor four-leggeds about, but the broken fence might explain that riddle.

"Wynn! Stop! You big fool! You'll do yourself a grave mischief, you will." The shouting came from the other side of the barn.

Kingsley and Algar picked up their pace. As they rounded the corner, a monk was pitted in a hopeless battle against an immense bay draft horse. The horse was intent upon devouring a pale-hued pile upon the ground. The Brother tugged at Wynn's halter with as much success as if he had been a fly.

Algar sniffed the air and his brows knit. "Apples?"

"T'would explain the horse's determination."

"Ah!" the monk exclaimed, his voice drenched in relief. "Good sirs, would you help me shift this horse? He is eager for the pomace, but a glut of it will cause him much ill."

"Of course, of course." Algar chuckled.

He took the horse's lead from the monk and clucked at the animal, to no avail.

"His name is Wynn," the monk offered.

"Chuck, chuck, Wynn!" Algar slapped the great beast with the end of the lead. Wynn ignored him, gobbling instead at the mass of crushed apples.

Kingsley stretched out his hand. "Here. Hand me over the rope. You go to the other side and push."

"Me! Why must I wade into the mush?"

"It is an opportunity to prove your strength and virility, is it not? None would think you past your prime if you could get this mountain of a horse to move his feet."

Algar pursed his lips but waded into the mass of apple pulp and laid his hands upon the hip of the workhorse. He slipped and scrambled, digging trenches and valleys with his boots in the fruity muck.

"Help me pull, Brother." Kingsley shifted his grip further up the rope so the monk could grab on.

"That's what's left of the apples from the cider press. There was a heavy harvest this year, and Wynn cannot master his desire for them."

At last, Algar's struggles yielded fruit. Wynn raised one massive hoof and Algar forced him to take a sidestep away from his sickly treat. That one shift in balance allowed Kingsley and the monk to pull the horse's head around. Accepting defeat, he glumly plodded next to the monk toward his stable.

Kingsley clenched his jaw to stop himself from laughing at his companion. Fermenting apple sauce was smeared from his boots to his waist. A chunk of apple core dangled from his hair.

"Our visit to Lord Thackere must need wait. You have desperate need of the laundress."

Algar shook his head, dislodging the core. And then he stopped, staring at the pomace. "God's bones!"

Kingsley's eyes followed his. A pale hand protruded from the soggy sleeve of a tattered cassock, which disappeared under the crushed apples.

He sighed. "I fear we have located Brother Mordecai."

"Poor soul." Algar made the sign of the cross. "Shall I go and fetch the abbot?"

"The state you're in? Beseems he already begrudges us the scant rations he grants at supper. We should be relocated to the stables with old Wynn, ere you track such muck into his chambers. I shall summon our unhappy host. As you are already in close acquaintance with the pomace, kindly remove Brother Mordecai from its wet embrace."

Algar scowled at his companion and turned to face the corpse, muttering under his breath.

"I return anon." Kingsley hurried toward the abbey.

Brother Camdyn, the Sacrist, gasped as his eyes fell upon Brother Mordecai. "The sacrilege!"

"Very bad luck to kill a man of the cloak, 'tis said." Algar stroked his chin.

"You speak true, but that is our holy relic, the dagger of Saint Ethelbert! To commit the cardinal sin of murder with such an item? That is true evil."

The three men stared at the jeweled handle that jutted from below Brother Mordecai's breastbone.

Kingsley was the first to speak. "Were there gouts of blood underneath the pomace? It has fallen in upon itself where it was heaped over the brother's body when you pulled it free."

"None that I saw. He is stiff as a timber, though."

Kingsley shot Algar a dirty look. "I'm sorry, Brother Camdyn. Old soldiers are jaded by the sight of corpses."

"I meant no disrespect, Brother."

Four monks approached the group, two of them bearing a litter to ferry their fallen comrade back to the holy halls.

When they arrived back in the infirmary, Wybert's casket lay on a wooden table at the center of the hall. There were no fragrant flowers to perfume the air, but the chill slowed the corpse's inevitable rot.

Brother Camdyn reached toward the jeweled haft of the dagger.

"Wait!" Kingsley raised his hand. He cast his eyes to Wybert's coffin. "Unwind his shroud."

"What! You would have us defile the dead?"

"No, Brother Camdyn. Young Wybert was stabbed with an unknown blade. We have the instrument of Brother Mordecai's death. I mean to see if the wounds match. The same villain might have dispatched them both."

Camdyn scowled, then waved his hand toward the wooden box. "Let it be done."

Two younger monks looked at him askance but lifted the lid and began their grim task.

Kingsley carefully withdrew the blade from Mordecai's corpse and studied the wound, marking its width to the second knuckle on his index finger. When the linen wrapping was cleared from Wybert's chest, he transferred his study there, the monks behind him frowning and shaking their heads.

After some moments, Kingsley's eyes sought Algar's. "The size of the blade is the same, as is the angle of the wound. An upward thrust from below the breastbone into the heart. The two were likely murdered by the same hand, methinks."

Algar shrugged. "Perhaps. And yet this dagger is a common size, and that method of killing is well known."

"Forsooth. But I reckon it is the more likely that they were slain by the same blackguard—it would be an odd coincidence for two citizens of the same abbey to be murdered in the same manner with the same type of blade by two different killers, would it not?" Kingsley handed the blood-stained dagger over to Brother Camdyn.

"I concede it is so." Algar turned his gaze to the Sacrist. "Did Brother Mordecai have any quarrel with his brethren? Or with the village folk?"

Camdyn shook his head. "None that I am aware. He was a gentle soul, well-liked and to my knowledge, had not an enemy upon this Earth."

Ah, but he had one. The good brother did not bury himself in that pomace. Kingsley pursed his lips. "Were Postulant Wybert and Brother Mordecai close friends? Did they conduct similar labors for the abbey?"

Brother Camdyn looked to each of the other monks, save the two busy re-wrapping Wybert's poor body. When none offered to speak, he replied. "They were no closer than any other of our Brothers, nor did they quibble. All monks work together, in one capacity or another."

One of the body-wrapping monks replaced the lid on the casket. "Brother Mordecai was the abbey's treasurer. As such, he oft sent postulants and novices upon errands in the village. Most often to the market."

"Was Wybert on such an endeavor the day of his death?"

"I know not." The young monk looked to Brother Camdyn.

The sacrist shook his head. "There was no need for Brother Mordecai to announce such trifling things to all of us."

Algar rubbed his jaw. "Is not the manor house of Lord Thackere beyond the apple orchard where young Wybert was slain? Perhaps he journeyed there for the Twelfth Night Feast with his kin."

Camdyn shook his head. "The abbot would not have approved such a foray. As you have seen, he does not set aside the vow of poverty for any feast or festival, even though the abbey could well afford such a luxury. Wybert had taken no vows as yet, but Father Cuthbert set his rules on all under the shelter of the abbey's roof, clergy or not."

"The excursion may not have been sanctioned, but perhaps Wybert undertook it nonetheless." Algar laid a hand on his stomach, as if recalling the miserable meal of the previous evening.

"Brother Camdyn?" Kingsley's mouth twitched into a vague smile. "What know you of wyverns?"

"Little. I do not subscribe to such fictions. And even if there were such a thing, it would not dare to set a single wicked foot upon the consecrated ground of the abbey."

"Then what make you of the tale of the wassailing party? Something abjured them from their ritual." Kingsley set his eyes expectantly upon those of the sacrist.

"As well they should turn from heathen customs!" Camdyn snorted. "But I did not witness the event, thus I cannot report what happened. Now, if you are done with your hinderance, we shall prepare Brother Mordecai's body for the grave."

Kingsley smiled through clenched teeth and gave the merest of bows. "We shall take our leave of you, then. We've errands of our own to pursue in regard to this ghastly business." He started to turn, then halted. "Has anyone been sent to fetch Sheriff Blackwoode?"

Camdyn's thin eyebrow arched. "The abbot has sole jurisdiction on these grounds and will inform Blackwoode if he deems it necessary."

Kingsley nodded and resumed his rotation. "Come, Algar. Our horses need to stretch their legs."

Once they were on the path to the stables, Algar elbowed his friend. "And what errand are you setting us upon?"

"We shall seek out Eadwulf Blackwoode so to deliver the news of Brother Mordecai's demise, and we should aim to return in time for the funeral of Wybert Thackere."

Sheriff Blackwoode had journeyed to the far end of the county, so Kingsley and Algar left word of the second murder with one of Eadwulf's underlings. By the time they had turned their horses on the path to the abbey, heavy, wet clumps of snowflakes had begun to fall from swollen clouds.

As they neared the apple orchard, Algar lifted the lower edge of his hood a little. "Is that a fire?" He pointed to the trees.

Kingsley turned his eyes in that direction. Something red clung to one of the biggest trees. "Not a fire, my friend. Let us make haste."

They coaxed their horses into a canter until they reached the gate. Kingsley stretched out his arm, cautioning Algar, before reining his own grey gelding down to a walk. "We must not frighten it away."

The collecting snow muffled the thud of horses' hooves upon the hard-packed ground. As they approached the very tree underneath which the body of Wybert Thackere had been found, the armored and scaly head of a red wyvern poked out of a hollow in the ancient trunk.

"God's bones!" Algar reached for his blade.

"Stay your hand! It is but a young one and I doubt it means us any harm. Do not slay it unprovoked. The creature may yet yield us some clue to Wybert's murder."

Algar grunted and dropped his arm. The horses halted of their own accord, ears pricked forward and nostrils flaring. The winged creature appeared to be climbing out of the hollow trunk but seemed to be held fast by something inside. The undersized dragon squawked and flapped its batlike wings as it struggled to take to the air.

"Mayhap its tail is stuck in a split of the tree." Algar pulled his cowl tighter around his neck.

The heavy clots of snow had given way to smaller, dryer flakes that fell thicker and faster. Algar's chestnut mare stamped her foot and swished her tail. The wyvern's head snapped in their direction. It redoubled its struggles, then shot into the sky, quickly disappearing into the low clouds, alarming the horses.

Kingsley soothed his grey with soft words and a pat on the shoulder. "As kith and kin to dragons, wyverns have the same nose for treasure. Shall we go and sus out what has attracted it?"

Both horses were loath to move forward, so the riders dismounted and led the reluctant equines to the tree. Kingsley held the reins of both while Algar peered into the hollow, then reached in to withdraw an object. He had to twist it round, for it was too long to pass broadside through the hole.

"God's blood!" he swore as he held aloft a jeweled dagger. "Why would Brother Camdyn hide the murdering blade in this tree?"

"Why indeed?" Kingsley studied the knife. "It matches my recollection of the Dagger of St. Ethelbert, the same as drawn from Brother Mordecai's corpse."

"As I said before, it is ill luck to murder a clergyman. Mayhap his pious blood has cursed the steel and Brother Camdyn hid the relic away to keep others from harm?"

Kingsley frowned and shook his head. "This small hollow is not a suitable lair for the dragonet we saw—why did it seek out the dagger in this tree the day before Brother Mordecai was killed? The abbot would hardly store their cherished relic in someone else's orchard. No, something else must have drawn it hither."

"Forsooth. Let me give these reins over to you for a moment."

Algar took the leather strips in one hand, while he examined the blade he held in the other. Kingsly stuck his head in the tree hole, then pulled it out and plunged his arm therein to the shoulder. After some time had passed, he was rewarded with the sound of wood scraping on wood.

"See here!" Kingsley grunted as he hauled a heavy leather pouch out of the hollow bore. "There is a false bottom to this hiding place." He raised the bag. "There are more like it in this cache."

The horses had settled, and Algar felt it safe to tie them to a low branch of the aged apple tree. The old soldiers knelt upon the ground to examine their finds more closely.

Kingsley unbuckled the strap that held the leather purse closed. Out spilled a hoard of coins, some gold, but most silver. A small silk pouch was closed with a drawstring. The soldier unbound it and poured sparkling jewels into the palm of his hand.

"This is what the wyvern coveted." Kingsly poured the gemstones back into their luxurious bag. "But who has stashed it thus? Remember you the silver coin under the hand of poor, dead Wybert? Had he found the treasure and lost his life for it? A hoard such as this might rival his brothers' wealth, and he could forgo the abbey's ungentle shelter. The one who hid the treasure might have taken violent exception to his plundering it."

Algar gathered the coins back into the leather purse, pausing to examine one here and there. "That could be so. Or it may be that on his excursion from the abbey, he chanced upon someone hiding their ill-gotten gains. A highwayman perhaps? Or the comely maid who bade us seek not the wyvern?"

"And yet, how would either come by this relic?" Kingsley pointed to the dagger that now lay near the pouch. "And slay Brother Mordecai with the selfsame dagger? Surely the abbot kept it housed in the chapel's reliquary."

"You suspect one of the monks?"

"Or someone familiar to them."

Kingsley's gelding nickered, and the men looked up. An elderly woman in a dark cloak grinned at them, then used her cane for balance as she stooped to pick up a silver penny that Algar had missed.

"Grandmother! We did not hear you coming!" Kingsley got to his feet. "Do you live nearby? We can escort you to your hearth fire so your bones don't freeze in this snow."

She chuckled. "My home is very near here, and I don't need your coddling." She flipped the coin into the air and caught it—her gnarled fingers surprisingly nimble—before slipping it inside her cloak. "I reckon you two had best get back to your own shelter before the snowfall buries the road. Did you not feel the rise in the wind? The stronger bite of the cold? I've no room for such burly carles in my house. Hie thee hence."

Even as she spoke, the snow began to fall thicker. The orchard gate was scarcely visible from where they stood.

Kingsley fancied he'd caught a glint of silver beneath the crone's hood but couldn't be certain if it was metal or glossy hair. "Wise words, Grandmother. Can we not help you get out of this weather?"

"I need no help, but *you* might, if you tarry. Your horses will know the way to their grain. Fly, you fools!"

Algar untied the reins, while Kingsley fixed the leather purse to his saddle.

Before he set his foot in the stirrup, Kingsley turned to the old woman. "Thank you, Grandmother. Be warm tonight."

Algar swung his leg over his mount. "Fare thee—"

The "well" died on his tongue. The woman no longer stood next to the old tree.

The snow was only a few inches deep, but rapidly building. Kingsley and Algar spurred their horses into a fast trot, hurrying to the abbey before the roads became impassable.

Algar rubbed his arms as he paced Kingsley's hostelry cell. Kingsley had wrapped himself in his woolen blanket and shivered on his bed.

"Now what shall we do?" Algar paused to blow warm breath into his hands. "We are no closer to capturing the killer, though we might have his motive."

"We must—"

Three quiet taps sounded upon his door.

"Who goes there?" Algar, who was already next to the entryway, asked.

"Brother Camdyn," came a hushed voice.

Algar pulled on the brass handle and admitted the monk to the chamber.

"I have need of your advice."

"Pray tell us what has happened, Brother." Kingsley got to his feet.

"I do not know if I have been blessed with a miracle or cursed by a trick of the Devil himself."

Algar's brow furrowed. "Do tell."

With a trembling hand, Camden reached beneath his cloak and withdrew a dagger. The Dagger of Ethelbert. Algar's mouth fell open.

"After I cleaned this up and re-consecrated it in the chapel, I went to return it to the reliquary. But our holy relic was still in its resting place. How? How came there to be two Daggers of Ethelbert?"

Kingsley and Algar locked eyes. Kingsley slid his hand beneath his pillow to retrieve the weapon they had discovered hidden in the old tree. "Three Daggers of Ethelbert."

The monk steadied himself with a hand against the wall and drew his trembling hand across his brow. "Whence did you find this?"

"An agéd tree in the apple orchard has a hollow, and it was stashed therein." Algar crossed his arms.

"The orchard? Where the postulant was found?" The brother laid his hand upon his chest.

"Brother Camdyn, take us to the reliquary." Kingsley let fall the woolen blanket from his shoulders onto the cot.

The monk led them quickly to the chapel, via a less-traveled route. This avoided some of the hubbub, as the abbey had opened its doors to the poor and unhoused to shelter from the snowstorm. When the trio arrived at their destination, Camdyn closed and barred the doors, then handed Algar a torch before removing the lid of the ornate wooden box that housed the holy dagger. It lay inside its case, firelight glinting off the red stones in the hilt.

"At least two of these are forgeries." Kingsley set his bejeweled blade on the altar next to the reliquary.

Camdyn did the same.

Kingsley raised his gaze from the triplet blades. "Algar, lend me the torch."

He handed it over. Kingsley held the flame as close as he dared to the daggers. He moved the fire to examine the weapons from diverse angles.

At last, he nodded. "The garnets in these two," he indicated the dagger he and Algar had discovered and the one provided by

Brother Camdyn, "are made of glass. Bubbles may be seen here and here." He pointed to a stone on each dagger.

The monk closed his eyes and bowed his head. "It is as I feared, then. Father Cuthbert makes many a journey into the village and he oft takes with him a leather purse of coins. He claims he distributes them amongst the poor, but he refuses any company on such trips. Had young Wybert, on his ill-conceived pilgrimage to the manor, chanced upon him hiding the stolen money in the tree? Mayhap the abbot slew him to still his tongue."

"And how came he by this false relic?" Algar frowned.

"The abbey makes a fair profit on the sale of holy relics to pilgrims at the hostelry. It shames me to think he has knowingly traded in forgeries."

Kingsley ran a hand through his sable locks. "And what of Brother Mordecai? He seemed to have no quarrel with Father Cuthbert ere his murder."

Camdyn traced the hilt of the closest dagger with a finger. "Brother Mordecai, God rest his soul, was the abbey treasurer. It would fall to him to confront Father Cuthbert if the accounts did not tally."

Algar nodded and crossed his arms. "Yes. It stands to reason that if the abbot had slain the boy, the next murder would be easier for him."

"The abbot's devotion to penury is a mark against him, if it is merely a pretense." Kingsley handed the torch back to Algar. "Brother Camdyn, can you tell of the Father's whereabouts on the morning Wybert was murdered?"

"I spoke with him at matins but did not see him at lauds. And he was late for prime."

Kingsley sighed and sought Algar's eyes. "It is a sad business. Brother Camdyn, lead us to Father Cuthbert."

The three men proceeded to the abbot's offices in silence. Without ceremony, the monk flung open the door, then gasped, raising his hand to his mouth.

The abbot sat in his chair, a girl of about ten on his lap. Their heads both whipped in the direction of the offending door.

Father Cuthbert's jaw clenched, and his lips pressed into a thin line. "It is customary to knock before entering my chambers." He eased the child onto her feet. "Go to your mother."

"But Father…"

"Do not worry. Go."

As the girl scurried away, Brother Camdyn glowered at his superior. "What, sir, is the meaning of this?"

The abbot got to his feet. "How dare you barge into my private office! This insubordination shall not go unmarked."

"Father." Kingsley's voice was calm but commanding. "It is not my place to settle quarrels within your house. I ask you to set it aside and continue it anon, if you see fit. As agents of the bishop, we are duty bound to investigate the murders of Postulant Wybert and Brother Mordecai, and I require information from you."

"Of me! I have the bishop's ear, you know. Tread carefully, sir."

"An innocent man has no need of threats."

The abbot scowled at the invaders of his office for a long moment. "Get on with it, then."

Kingsley swallowed, choosing his queries to the wily abbot carefully. "On the morning of Wybert Thackere's death, you missed lauds and were late to prime. Wh—"

"Churl!" the abbot lashed out at Brother Camdyn. "Are you spreading rumor and gossip behind my back?"

Algar stepped in front of the monk, as if to shield him from the abbot's ire.

Kingsley remained unflappable. "I must inquire of your whereabouts on that day."

"You must do nothing, save pay taxes and die. Get out of my office and consider yourself lucky that I shall allow you to remain in the hostelry until the storm breaks."

With a grim smile upon his lips, Kingsley strode forth and sat himself in a chair across from the abbot.

"The bishop shall hear of your insolence," the abbot snarled.

"Perhaps. But so shall he hear of your refusal to aid in our inquest."

The two locked eyes for a seemingly interminable time.

The abbot picked up a quill. "My errands are my own. I did not encounter young Wybert, much less murder him."

"Can any vouch for you?"

"The church trusts me to administer this abbey. Is my word not good enough for an impertinent soldier?"

"Alas, I would that it were." Kingsley eyed a silver penny that glinted on the abbot's desk.

"What know you of the apple tree's secret?"

Father Cuthbert blinked. "I am no farmer." He leaned back in his chair, his sullen eyes on Kingsley.

"Where do you take the money? I am given to understand that you leave with pouches of coins as alms and return with none. And yet the village poor are still poor."

"Father!" The young girl ran back into the room, straight to the abbot. "I cannot find Mummy." Tears flooded from her green eyes.

Kingsley cocked his head. The abbot also had green eyes.

"I beg your pardon, Father. You are guilty of avarice and breaking your vows to the church, but you slew no one." Kingsley got to his feet. "Algar, seize Brother Camdyn. It was his hand that laid low both Postulant Wybert and Brother Mordecai. Father, you must send for Sheriff Blackwood posthaste."

"What? Unhand me!" Camdyn snarled at Algar.

"Brother Camdyn? What say you to this charge?" Father Cuthbert rose from his chair.

"Do not dare to feign righteousness with me." Camdyn's low voice dripped with venom. "You knew as well as I that the relics you sold to pilgrims were forgeries and were glad enough to pocket your share of the money. How much of it did you spend on your secret family? Three children and a wife require no small means of upkeep."

Cuthbert put his arm around the girl's shoulders, then bent and spoke softly to her. "Cerelia, my dear daughter. Make your way to the refectory and ask Brother Swithin for some bread. He will not refuse you. Ask him to send one of the novices to fetch the sheriff. I shall meet you there anon."

She sniffled and nodded, then retreated from the chamber.

The abbot dropped into his chair and fixed his eyes upon Kingsley. "How did you reckon Cerelia was my daughter? And why think you that Brother Camdyn is a murderer?"

Kingsley took a step forward. "When I noticed that she had the same eyes as you, I realized that when she had called you 'Father,' it was not in the ecclesiastical sense. When we found her sitting in your lap, it would have been unseemly for an abbot, but common enough for a parent. She was in no way distressed, but comfortable."

Cuthbert nodded and sighed. "She is but eleven summers, and already her mother is pushing me to make a goodly match for her. I feel she is far too young to wed. She knows nothing of our strife, and yet her cousin only two summers older has been married off to the son of a merchant the next village over. Cerelia must surely be aware the days of her childhood are numbered. I had set aside money for her dowry, to ensure a quality husband."

His words were like a dagger between Kingsley's ribs. His own daughter had been stillborn, and his heart-broken wife died of a fever only days after. He'd fled that tragedy and become a soldier, but never stopped grieving his lost family.

"And why do you accuse me?" Camdyn growled, shaking the grip of Kingsley's memories.

"When you came to us with your tale of the duplicate dagger, Algar told you we found another like it secreted in a hollow apple tree. He made no mention of hidden coins, and yet you put forward the idea that Father Cuthbert slew the boy over that self-same money. So eager were you to cast Father Cuthbert in front of the oxcart, as it were, that your own actions became suspect. Despite your vigorous pretense to the contrary, you knew full well we had obtained the second forged dagger because you yourself left it for us to find."

The monk glowered but said nothing. Algar rubbed his chin with his free hand and nodded.

Kingsley continued.

"We were told that novices and postulants alike were at the disposal of Brother Mordecai for the running of errands. You yourself remarked that as treasurer, it would fall on him to confront the abbot should the balances not align. I surmised that the income from the sale of the faux relics did not make its way to the abbey's coffers, and Brother Mordecai, loath to hurl accusations without proof, sent young Wybert to follow the abbot on his mysterious forays into the village."

Cuthbert hung his head. "I should have guessed as much when poor Wybert was discovered in the orchard. It seemed an odd coincidence he should be found 'neath the very tree that held my secret stash. Brother Camdyn accompanied me as far as the orchard. He had happened upon a new forger of relics and wished to show me the daggers he had acquired. I had no ken of a wyvern haunting the orchard." He sighed. "Brother Mordecai was not the dalcop, even if I accused him of being a fool."

"And yet the wyvern is the very thing that led us to find the false relic and your cache of treasure." Algar added an emphatic nod.

"Brother Camdyn, I know not whether Brother Mordecai confided in you or confronted you. Either way, you knew the secret of your relic peddling would not long hold. You had to act in haste to conceal his body, and so left the dagger therein to be hidden when you moved his corpse to a more permanent location."

Camdyn's mouth flopped open and snapped shut.

"Did I not say to you that selling these ersatz Daggers of Ethelbert was a risky venture?" Cuthbert's eyes fell upon his criminal colleague. "Now the lives of a young man and a worthy monk have been cut unnaturally short and we are both ruined. The bishop, no doubt, will seize the money, and Cerelia will have nothing for her dowry."

"We would have been rich men, had it not been for these meddlesome carles!" Brother Camdyn bit Algar suddenly and hard.

The soldier yelped in surprise and pain, releasing his grip on the monk's wrist. Brother Camdyn fled down the corridor. It took only a moment for Kingsley and Algar to recover their wits and charge after him.

An "oof!" and sounds of a scuffle came from around the corner.

"Stop that monk!" Kingsley had the presence of mind to shout. "Murderer!"

When they turned into the next hallway, they found Sheriff Blackwoode and a handful of his men in custody of the killer clergyman.

"It was Brother Camdyn who slew Wybert and Mordecai," Kingsly panted.

"How came you to arrive so soon to the abbey?" Algar inquired of the sheriff. "The novice was only just sent to fetch you."

"We were scarcely outside the gate when we met him upon the road. We had been advised by the scorned wife of a metalsmith who had taken some scandalous ecumenical commissions. After we called upon him at his smithy, he quickly confessed and relinquished to us the names of several high-ranking clergy who purchased his unsavory wares. As Brother Camdyn was on the list, we came forthwith to the abbey."

After the office of vespers was completed, supper was served. The monks murmured amongst themselves over their scant trenchers. Even though the abbot had relaxed his death grip from the abbey's purse strings, what food there was in the buttery had to be shared with the hungry villagers who were sheltering from the storm. The refectory was surprisingly peaceful. There was no evidence of the baleful wight that had been afflicting the place when they arrived.

"Do you suppose the ghostly rampage has finished?" Algar asked between mouthfuls of bread.

"It seems appeased, now that the murderer has been caught and the abbot's duplicity has been brought to light." Kingsley's thoughts went to the strange woman from the market who had told him that if they found the murderer, the sprite would cease its violence.

Algar set his beaker of cider on the table with a loud thump. "You reckon the bishop will reward us for recovering all that money?"

A silent Kingsley watched the abbot's daughter playing with two younger boys, probably her brothers. Algar followed his eyes and sighed.

Kingsley turned toward his companion. "Father Cuthbert is a favorite of the bishop. He will likely face little consequence. Many a church pads their income with trade in holy relics, though I ween the bishop might care to keep that part of our adventure out of the public eye. He would be content with some of the spoils, though."

"Some?"

"Any house that can afford gold candlesticks can afford to pay the dowry for a young bride. That money likely means the difference between her finding a successful husband or no husband. It is a hard life for a woman alone. I propose we take the purse of money we have discovered to the bishop and leave the rest."

"And you trust the deceitful abbot to administer this dowry?"

"Did you not see how tender he was with the girl? I am willing to leave the matter to the Fates."

Algar shrugged. "Very well, then. I am ready to return to the bishop with tomorrow's sunrise. Perhaps God will smile upon your generosity with other people's money and put the fair maiden we chanced upon in the apple orchard in our path."

"I doubt that indeed."

"Because you eschew the company of beautiful women is no reason I should."

"Algar, I fear she is no woman of flesh and bone. I wager she is some spirit of this place, or perhaps an avenging angel, ensuring justice for the deaths of innocents. I reckon she is more than she seems and would swiftly put paid to your amorous attempts."

"I wished to savor the sweet beauty of this young woman, and you offer me up a nursery bogey." Algar raised his beaker to his lips.

Kingsley lifted his own mug. *Godspeed, Brother Mordecai, Postulant Wybert. It is a pity your trusted brother was rotten to the core.*

Outside came the distant caw of a single crow. To Kingsley's ear, it seemed to be laughing.

REFLECTION
By A. B. Richards

I HATE office Christmas parties with the heat of a thousand suns. Especially my husband's. Oh, sure, the company spared no expense on the buffet. The waitstaff were adorable in their red vests and Santa hats. The hotel had placed different colored artificial trees about every twenty feet around the ballroom. Red trees twinkled with white lights, green trees with red, and silver trees with blue. *Humbug*.

I'd been left to fend for myself. First, it was the CIO who wanted Clifton to step outside and smoke a cigar or two.

As soon as he came in from that, it was time for the 'awards' ceremony. They were supposed to be good humored and funny—like Meredith Hatcher getting the Oxygen Boost award—including a $20 gift card—because of the array of potted plants that threatened to overrun her office. I'd met her a few times. She seems very nice.

Clifton was one of the presenters. Linda Peters was his co-presenter. I can't *prove* that they're sleeping together. Clifton swears they aren't. But I don't need a Magic 8 Ball to know that signs point to yes.

Someone tsk'd behind me. I turned to see a woman who looked like she'd stepped off the red carpet at some blockbuster movie premiere. Her dress was a stunning retro—embroidered flowers on the barely opaque sheath dress accented her curves.

I suddenly felt even more out of place. I am reasonably fit, but four pregnancies are going to leave their marks, aren't they? *Maybe I should have just stayed home with the kids.*

"What? No seafood mousse tonight?" The stunning woman placed her manicured hands on her slim hips.

I tried to be helpful. "They had some shrimp cocktails over at the appetizer bar."

"Hmmm. If I got a single drop of that red sauce on this dress, the whole thing would be ruined, right?"

"Maybe. But then you'd just have to use it to create your own design elements." I couldn't imagine anyone being able to eat anything in that dress.

She laughed. "Devastatingly practical, I see. By the by, I'm Sylvia."

Do we shake hands now? She didn't extend hers, so I left mine at my side. "Beverly."

"Marvy, darling."

The live band had left the stage. Clifton and Linda were walking up the three short steps onto it.

Sylvia shook her head. "Not this again."

"Yeah. When you don't know any of these people, these inside joke awards are kinda boring." I couldn't take my eyes off Clifton, though.

"You look kinda bummed. What's wrong?" She followed my eyes to the stage, where Clifton and that woman seemed to be having the time of their lives. "That's your old man, isn't it?"

I nodded.

Sylvia's eyes narrowed. "They seem pretty tight."

"Yeah…"

"Look, I have a real jones for a puff right now. You wanna go up on the roof with me?"

What are my options? Watch my husband laugh and joke with a woman almost half his age, or watch a random stranger smoke a cigarette. "Sure. Why not?"

The holiday decorations and lights sparkled joyfully in downtown Houston as the glass elevator crawled up a floor to the top of the building. The hotel had made the most of their rooftop real estate. We stepped off the elevator into a covered atrium lined with lush plants. It was a bit chillier outside—mid-fifties, I guessed.

Traffic on the nearby freeway was white noise that blurred the edges of our words. Water vapor drifted above the heated pool, which was surrounded by lounge chairs and a few covered cabanas. A putting green with artificial turf lay past the pool and to their left. What appeared to be a dance floor was opposite that. A bar, closed for the evening, but still dressed in lurid neon, stood to the right of the pool, with a steaming hot tub in between.

I rubbed my arms against the chill. *Maybe we should go stand by the hot water.*

Snick. Snick.

I had no idea where the cigarette and lighter came from, but Sylvia pulled in a deep drag, then released the smoke.

She strolled over to one of the lounges by the pool and sat down, stretching out her long legs. Her dress was so shiny it looked wet. Sylvia took another pull on her cigarette, then patted the lounge next to her.

I sat, awkwardly. *My office-Christmas-party gown was not meant to be lounged in.*

Sylvia flicked ashes from the end of her cigarette. "My husband cheated on me, too. Big, fat louse."

Is it that obvious? "I'm sorry, Sylvia."

"He was so furious when I confronted him with it. He threw me into the pool." She gave a half laugh and took another drag.

"He sounds like a real piece of work."

"We should go swimming."

"What? It's too cold. Besides, I didn't bring a suit."

Sylvia laughed. "Pool's heated. There are towels over there." She tilted her head to a tiki hut by the hot tub. "Just take off what you don't want to get wet."

"You want to go skinny dipping? People have been coming up here all night to smoke, or whatever."

"They're watching their dopey awards. Nobody will be up here for a while."

"To be completely honest, I don't like water. I can't swim."

Sylvia took another puff, letting the smoke out slowly. "I can teach you."

I had only drunk half a glass of wine, so I couldn't blame it on the alcohol. Perhaps it was the pent-up need to do something fun, something spontaneous, with just a sprinkle of desire for revenge. If someone caught Sylvia and me naked in the pool together at the company Christmas party, Clifton would be the laughingstock of the office.

I struggled to my feet and slipped off my pumps. "Let's do it." I reached around and tugged at my zipper. Of course it would be stuck.

"Let me help."

I flinched and gasped at the iciness of Sylvia's fingers as they brushed the back of my neck. The zip peeled open smoothly at her touch. In a moment, I'd slipped out of my underthings and was making my shivery way to the pool steps. I made a detour to grab a couple of towels and dropped them on one of the lounges. Wet footprints led to the pool steps.

Sylvia was already in the water, floating face down, her long hair billowing around her like seaweed.

"Sylvia!" What do I do? I don't know first aid for drowning.

I waded toward her, but she rotated her body and planted her feet on the bottom of the pool. She threw her head back and dipped it in the water to get the hair out of her face.

"Sorry, darling. I didn't mean to scare you."

The gleam in her eye suggested otherwise, but I wasn't going to argue about it.

The water was gloriously warm, and I wanted to submerge myself in it all the way up to my chin. But I didn't dare go that deep. Up to my armpits was as far as I was willing to go. I jumped. Something cold had brushed against my leg. Try as I might, I found nothing in the water.

"This is easy as pie." Sylvia stood next to me. "Take a deep, deep breath and hold it. Push off the bottom of the pool and raise your legs."

"I'm not really comfortable—"

"I'm here. I won't let anything happen to you. "

Sucking in even more air, I pushed off the bottom of the pool... and floated. I had goose flesh where the cold air touched my wet skin, but most of me was submerged in warm water. It wasn't too bad, actually.

The door to the atrium opened.

Oh, crap.

I let out the air I was holding and put my feet on the pool bottom, facing away from the oncoming footsteps. They stopped at the edge of the pool.

"Beverly?"

Of course it would be Clifton. Probably had set up a rendezvous with Little Miss Hot to Trot. "What are you doing out here?"

"I could ask you the same question. Dear."

Clifton walked around to the long side of the pool, so he was closer to where I stood at the border between the shallow and deep ends. A swirl of red twisted around me. I glanced at my arms and hands, then down my body. It was not coming from me. *And why was the water suddenly cold?*

"Why are you there? You don't swim."

"I can touch the bottom here." He took no notice whatsoever of Sylvia. She had moved against the wall, not far from where he stood.

Clifton stepped to the edge of the pool and leaned over, reaching for me. "How much have you had to drink? Come on. Let's get you out of there before anyone else comes out here."

"Are you expecting someone else?"

Before he could answer, Sylvia popped out of the water and grabbed his hand. I hadn't even registered what was happening as she pulled him to the bottom of the deep end.

"No! Sylvia, stop!"

There was nothing I could do to save Clifton, but perhaps someone else could. "Help! Help me, please!" I screamed as I plowed through the water to get out of the pool.

I wrapped a towel around myself and ran to the elevator. The car was still there, and I jumped inside.

I must have been quite the sight, running into the company Christmas party dripping wet and wrapped in a towel, screaming my head off.

The investigators did not believe me when I told them about Sylvia. They finally got tired of me talking about her and showed me the security camera footage. It plainly showed me reclining on a lounger, taking off my clothes and prancing around in all my shivering glory at the side of the pool, then getting in and floating around.

Alone.

Completely alone. Until Clifton arrived. He reached out, stumbled, and fell into the pool, then sank to the bottom. And you know the rest.

There was a strange glimmering swirl at the bottom, but the officer said that was just reflections of the lights, and it only looked like it was at the bottom.

Two days later, I got an envelope in the mail. It was typed and there was no return address. Curious, I opened it to find a photocopy of a newspaper clipping from December 18, 1964. It was the photo that stunned me. Sylvia looked into the camera from a full studio pose.

Basically, the story was that she and her husband were attending a company Christmas party. She caught him in the ladies' room, canoodling with his secretary. Their fight ended up on the roof. He slapped her, and she fell into the pool, hitting her head as she went in, and drowned.

The kids were all in bed. I stood in the living room, staring out the picture window at our own pool. The light behind me turned the glass into a hazy mirror, backed by inky sky. Just for a second, it seemed my hair was long, and I wore a shimmery vintage dress. I shook my head, and it was only me standing there in sweats and a tee-shirt. Wet footprints led between the pool and the house.

Is that a glimmer of swirling light at the bottom? No, I tell myself. That's just the reflection of the full moon.

I check the lock on the back door. Just in case.

THE GIFT OF TRAVEL
By A. B. Richards

"SHHHH." Elizabeth stroked her daughter's forehead. "It's gonna be okay."

"It hurts," Camile grunted through gritted teeth.

"I know, baby. She's almost got it."

"There we go!" The doctor pulled out an implant from Camile's lower back. She quickly poked it into a ball of putty and dropped it onto a pile of identical balls in a dingy old yogurt maker filled with warm water. "You have about three hours, give or take, before they notice the GPS coordinates are wonky. Good luck," she said from behind her surgical mask.

Sirens wailed in the distance, coming closer. None of the three so much as breathed until the sound faded away. Elizabeth swallowed hard, trying to tamp down the adrenaline-induced nausea.

She leaned over and kissed her fourteen-year-old's cheek, then watched as the doctor made four stitches to close the incision. Her hands were not quite as steady as they had been earlier.

"These sutures will dissolve on their own, no need to have them removed. I'm going to put a medicated bandage on it. Just watch for any swelling or drainage." She clipped the excess suture. "You ready for yours?"

"More than ready. This will be the best Christmas present I ever got." She climbed up on the table and lay face down.

Elizabeth flinched as the needle slipped into her skin and the local anesthetic burned before it numbed. She squeezed her eyes shut and tried to visualize what their new life would be like once they got across the border.

The Department of Family Security had started out by offering resources to struggling families, especially those with infertility issues. Any woman that took advantage of DFS-services received an implant. Just a little transponder that would help them track their hormone levels in real time to determine the most favorable treatment windows. And it did improve the live birth rate of the various fertility therapies.

After this success, they encouraged all women of child-bearing years to get one. No need to pee on a stick—just check the app on your phone!

It did make it more convenient for a lot of women to judge their most fertile days. And they knew sooner than ever if there was a bun in the oven. When the pace of implant insertions slowed down, they pitched it to older women to track their hormones as they approached menopause.

Most people didn't read the fine print and were unaware that there was also a GPS tracker included. And by the time the implant became a requirement for women to vote, it had become so routine that few questioned it. Girls got them when they turned ten, just like a standard vaccination.

And then everything changed. Companies started firing unmarried women and those who had not had at least one child before the age of twenty-eight. With no children, they were ineligible to receive federal benefits. The homeless population soared. With nothing to hold them down, they were the first to find a way out of the country. The infertile quickly followed. The suburban soccer moms were the last to get it. It wasn't until their teenage daughters were ripped from their arms that they started to wake up.

So many women had fled that a repopulation plan had been put in place. On a girl's fifteenth birthday, she was required to report to a Patriot Home. She would live there with other girls until she had produced three babies. Only then could she be released. Unless she was infertile. Those girls cared for the babies and performed maintenance around the Home. That's all they were considered good for. The suicide rate was so high they were considering lowering the age to fourteen. Camile's age.

Elizabeth shuddered, remembering That Day. Aralia was Camile's best friend, and she lived across the street. There was a cheerleading competition on her actual birthday, so her party was the next weekend after. They had just cut the cake when a knock came at the door. Before Aralia's mother could answer it, it was kicked in and soldiers in full tactical gear rushed through. Everyone started shouting and running around, trying to find a place to hide. The men must have locked in on Aralia's implant, because they went straight to the couch she had hidden behind and ripped it away from the wall. She screamed and struggled. One of the men gave her an injection and she went limp. They carried her away without a word. Her mother cried so hard she threw up. Elizabeth still had nightmares about it.

Thank goodness for the cartels. Elizabeth never in a million years thought she would say that. They had decades of experience smuggling drugs and migrant workers across the border. Now they were cashing in on smuggling women out of the country. Working with the cartel coyotes was expensive and dangerous. They were a criminal gang, not a troop of boy scouts. If anything went wrong, they would abandon you to your fate—no refunds. They might make demands Elizabeth couldn't bear to think about. And there was always the chance they'd shoot you in the dessert and leave you for the four-legged coyotes.

It had taken Elizabeth almost five years to secretly save the cash for their forged identification papers and the smugglers, plus traveling expenses. US dollars, Mexican pesos, and Vietnamese dong were stashed in small batches throughout their clothes and backpacks. If they got robbed, which was likely, they wouldn't lose all of it. She'd convinced her husband to leave a day early for his parents' house for Christmas, on account of Camile's alleged school activities. He probably would have helped, but she didn't want him to go to prison. It was best for everyone if he didn't know.

"Ow!" The implant was a little deeper than the reach of the anesthetic.

"Sorry." The doctor squirted more lidocaine into the incision.

Camile looked up from her phrase booklet.

Elizabeth hoped her smile was reassuring. "It's alright. I'm good."

"It'd be a lot easier with one of those language apps, Mom."

"I'm aware of that. But we can't leave any clues to where we're going. No way to trace a paper book. Bounty hunting has become too big of a business."

It wasn't painful, due to the anesthetic, but Elizabeth felt the doctor stitching her up, suture tugging on her skin. It seemed like a metaphor for her current situation—pulling her life together in a broken world. The medicated patch was cold on her back.

"I'm done. You can go. Make sure you go out the side door on the west side of the building. Same door you came in. Security camera there is offline."

"Thanks, doc." Elizabeth clasped the surgeon's gloved hand. She didn't know the doctor's name, and the doctor didn't know Elizabeth's and her daughter's. She worked for the New Underground Railroad, and that was enough of a credential.

Elizabeth and Camile made their way down the darkened hallway and into the dimly lit stairwell. A door opened somewhere and dropped closed, the metal slap echoing off the cement walls.

They froze. But when no footsteps sounded on the concrete stairs, they continued to the first floor and to the exit.

"Get back!" Elizabeth jerked Camile away from the small window in the door. A police cruiser crawled down the avenue, its spotlight raking the grounds with strident white light.

Elizabeth slid down the wall, her heart thudding so hard against her ribs she was sure it would break through her chest.

She checked her watch, an old-school analog. "The driver will be here in ten minutes," she whispered. "I hope the cops are long gone by then."

The women waited inside until a dark grey sedan pulled up to the curb. It was the car Elizabeth was expecting.

"Camile? If anything happens, run. As hard and fast as you can. Better to get shot and bleed out in the street than go back."

Camile looked at the floor and nodded.

The driver would be wearing a disguise, for everyone's safety. Elizabeth peered through the window. As she crept out the door hand-in-hand with Camile, she scanned the entire road and crossed her fingers that the driver hadn't been compromised.

Camile and Elizabeth dropped their backpacks on the seat and sat on the floor, backs against the doors. It was uncomfortable, but it would keep them unnoticed.

They rode in silence for almost half an hour. Tinsel garlands, exuberant twinkling lights, and six-foot plastic nutcracker soldiers flashed past the windows for the first few blocks. The decorations became more sparse as they drove, then petered out altogether. The glimpse of a Christmas tree in a second-story window was like a knife in Elizabeth's heart. Her own tree back home was dark tonight, and the pile of presents, all clothed in glossy paper, waited for a celebration that would never come.

The car lurched to a stop. "We're here. Good luck."

"Thank you."

Elizabeth couldn't tell if the voice was male or female. If they were at the right place, she didn't much care. Camile waved once as the vehicle pulled away.

A security light at the far corner of the roof cast a sallow glow on the cracked pavement. The long, blocky building looked like a warehouse. They could be in any one of the dozens of industrial office/warehouse developments around the city. This one was definitely in a seedier part of town.

A door opened nearby. "Carol? Lucy?"

Elizabeth had forgotten that was her new name and hesitated to respond.

"That's us," Camile replied.

Their new last name was Ashford. Elizabeth, now Carol, thought it would be easy to remember. Their old life was nothing but ashes, but they would rise like phoenixes.

They walked the grimy door, and a Hispanic woman led them through the small office section and into the warehouse.

Ten other women, clumped in small, nervous groups, waited next to a heavy-duty pickup attached to a flatbed trailer loaded with appliance boxes.

"If you need to go to the bathroom, do it now. It's going to be a long ride." The woman who had met them at the door pointed back toward the offices.

Carol and Lucy trotted over to the filthy one-seater broom-closet-sized restroom and did what they needed to do. When they returned, the other women were gone.

"Hurry up!" a man with a tattoo of an ornately decorated skull in front of a marijuana leaf on his arm snarled at them and gestured to the trailer. It was then Carol noticed two women standing on a square of cardboard on an outside row of crates.

The one in a blue track suit beckoned. "You're with us. Come on."

Carol and Lucy stepped onto the cardboard, and someone lowered the top of a refrigerator box over the four women. There was no room to sit, only stand, and each wall of the box had an air hole. Carol's faced the cab of the truck and Lucy's the boxes in the middle. The woman in the blue track suit lucked out—her air hole looked out on the road. Lengths of cotton webbing had been stapled around the box, presumably for the women to hold onto if the ride got rough.

Hours had passed, and Carol's feet hurt so badly she wanted to cry. She was cold and hungry and just about at the end of her rope. The anesthetic had worn off long ago, and her surgical wound throbbed. The women had hardly spoken—riding in the trailer on the highway was noisy. The woman in the blue track suit kept them posted on landmarks, but it was dark outside and there wasn't much to see most of the trip. Still, Carol would have traded places with her in a heartbeat.

The truck had slowed down but was still going forward. Carol guessed they were on the backroads now. After a while, they rolled to a stop. A truck door opened, and there were voices, but Carol couldn't make out the words over the engine.

After a short time, the voices got closer and closer until it sounded like the men stood next to the very box Carol and Lucy hid in.

"*Sí.* Just appliances, man. Why you hasslin' us?"

"You know why. Fuckin' wetback."

Carol held her breath, but she couldn't keep herself from trembling. A sound… familiar, but it still took a moment to identify.

Snuffling.

A dog barked. A deep throaty roar that could only come from a big dog.

Without warning, something slammed into the box, slashing the cardboard behind it, stopping suddenly with a wet smack. Warm liquid sprayed across Carol's face. The woman in the track suit moaned and gurgled as she slid to the bottom of the box.

Pop. Pop. Pop.

So loud. Like popcorn in the microwave turned up to eleven. Carol clapped hands over her ears, but she still heard the women screaming. She wondered if she was one of them. Here in the dark with the coppery stink of blood, she couldn't be sure of anything. The truck door slammed. Carol nearly lost her footing in the slick liquid that now covered the bottom of the box as the driver punched the accelerator and plowed through the roadblock. She was grateful for the cotton webbing that kept her upright. Barely.

Lucy reached out to her mother, touched the warm, sticky wetness, and gasped. She did not reach out again for the rest of the trip.

Fear has a smell—sharp and metallic, with hints of raw meat. It has a taste, too. Like garlic and copper. The box reeked of fear and blood so much that Elizabeth wanted to grab Camile's hand, throw off the box and run. The other woman in the crate with them cried. Elizabeth caught snatches of prayers from other containers. She had prayed so many times for Camile. For her friends' daughters who disappeared one by one into the livestock barns of the Patriot Homes. But God never answered, or His answer was another girl gone, so she gave up trying.

Bloodless grey was seeping over the eastern horizon when the truck stopped, and the exhausted women were unloaded from their appliance crates. The woman in the blue track suit and the red-stained box were loaded into the bed of another truck that drove away across the desert, kicking up dust that hovered like a trail of ghosts in its wake.

The third woman in the box sobbed and screamed as her friend disappeared.

"Shut up!" The driver raised a hand as if to slap her.

Lucy put her arm around the woman's waist and whispered in her ear.

Carol swallowed the last of the moisture in her mouth. "What happened?"

"Bounty hunters." He spat. "*¡Pendejos!* He had an ax. Thought he was gonna split open that box. We split *him* open." With a nasty cackle, he stalked away to a group of men struggling with a manhole cover.

When the cover was lifted, one of the men climbed down into the hole.

"Follow him." The driver pointed at the opening.

The women descended into the tunnel, like a line of Persephones entering the Underworld. The dried blood on Carol's skin cracked and flaked off as she moved. Her clothes stank. Blood. Sweat. Urine. There was nowhere to clean up.

The women ahead of them sloshed through the inches-deep foul-smelling water in the tunnel. Flickering and buzzing electric torches lit the narrow concrete tube but gave no warmth.

Carol was so thirsty that she considered drinking the muddy, filthy liquid that soaked her feet and the hem of her pants.

Lucy paused to pluck something from the reeking water. A little doll. She was missing an eye and her hair looked like she'd stuck a spoon in an electrical outlet. A tear ran down Lucy's face as she tucked it into her pocket.

What lay at the end of the tunnel? Death? Slavery? Freedom? When it was her turn to climb the iron rungs, she almost couldn't do it. As she put her hands on the bars, she realized her wedding ring was missing. "No!"

She whirled to go back to the truck, but the armed man behind her blocked her way. He jerked his head toward the metal bars. "*Arriba!*"

"You don't understand! It's the only thing I have from my husband."

He shoved her and she nearly tumbled into the water.

Lucy called down from the top, "Come on Mom! It's okay. Dad would understand."

He would. He'd always been good to her. She missed him. Her nice house in the suburbs. A hot shower. A pantry full of food. The lost ring was the final shedding of that old skin. Underneath was something raw and fierce. Something birthed in the flames that consumed her old life. Her old life had been happy and comfortable, though, and she had not wanted what she was being forced to become.

Carol sobbed softly as she put her foot on one rung and then the next. Soon, she stood with the Rio Grande at her back as the sun rose over the Chihuahuan Desert. Wispy mackerel clouds reflected pinks and purples across the rugged land that stretched away to the horizon. Juarez lay just to the west. It was nearly a straight shot down to the Port of Manzanillo, where they'd hop a container ship bound for Vietnam. The cartel controlled the entire territory, so she expected little drama.

Carol hugged her daughter. "Merry Christmas, baby."

They were free.

For now.

DONOR

By A. B. Richards

"Beppe, I'm not sure this is a good idea." Maisie rested her hand on her swollen abdomen.

"I know the timing isn't great. But it's Dad's first Christmas without Mom, and I can't not go. And I won't leave you all alone. We'll be home in plenty of time. You aren't due for another three weeks."

Maisie sighed. Her back constantly hurt, she got out of breath just walking across the room, and every time she lay down to sleep, the baby started kicking her in the diaphragm. It was tough enough being around her in-laws—especially Cousin Bianca—on a good day, much less for a week when she felt like something the cat dragged in. If a cat could drag a beached whale through the pet flap. But under the circumstances, what choice did she have?

She made a noncommittal noise and rolled down the window, just a few inches. He had the heat on. Sweat dripped down Maisie's forehead and into her eyes.

Viola—Beppe's mother, had been the family peacemaker, quashing quarrels, healing hurt feelings, and smoothing rough edges for the entire time Maisie had been in the family. Now, Lucia and Bianca would have no guardrails. *Quit stressing about it. Flooding your baby with cortisol is bad. Just breathe. It will be fine.*

"I need to make a pit stop soon."

"Again? We've stopped three times already."

Maisie shrugged. "It's not my fault I have to pee every thirty minutes. You try carrying the next one, huh?"

Beppe sighed, his shoulders slumping. "Okay. I'll take this exit coming up."

Three pit stops later, they pulled up in front of Rudolpho's house. Zia Lucia's white Mercedes was parked square in the middle of the driveway, taking up all four possible spaces. Another car—undoubtedly Bianca's—blocked the mailbox.

A net of green Christmas lights, barely visible in the afternoon sun, draped over an unevenly trimmed bush. A plastic wreath hung on the door.

Beppe retrieved their luggage from the trunk, and they made their way up the driveway.

Zio Emilio opened the door. "Beppe!" He hugged his nephew. "Maisie." He kissed her cheek. "Come on in."

Dripping with mostly costume jewelry, Zia Lucia luxuriated in an armchair like a queen holding court in the living room crowded with aunts, uncles, and cousins. Maisie knew at least half of them. Bianca and her husband Tony sat on the loveseat, the youngest two of their brood of four playing with soft toys on the carpet near their feet.

Beppe waved to the group. "I'll just drop the bags off—"

"Not so fast!" Bianca rose like a striking cobra. "We're taking the spare bedroom and we've put Treasure and Destiny in your old room."

Beppe scowled. "So, where are *we* supposed to sleep?"

Maisie hoped this meant they would be staying at a hotel, but didn't dare show it.

"Zia Viola isn't using her she-shed anymore. We thought that would be a cozy retreat for you. It's almost like a little house."

"Mama had that window unit for AC, but there's no heat out there." Beppe bent his elbows, his palms up in supplication.

Bianca leaned forward and ruffled the white-blond hair of her younger son. "But there is electricity. You can plug in a space heater."

"Is there one out there?"

"No."

"Beppe! Maisie!" Rudolpho and Uncle Carlo, who was the baby of that generation and never learned to speak Italian, came out of the kitchen and hugged each of the couple in turn. The golden aroma of baking bread made Maisie's stomach growl.

Rudolpho put his hands on her belly. "How's my youngest grandson?"

"Almost done cooking."

"Have you decided on a name yet?"

Beppe butted in. "Joshua."

"Did Lucia tell you? You're out in Viola's cottage. I thought it might be quieter for Maisie when she needs to rest."

"I'll have to run out and get a heater." Beppe jangled his car keys in his pocket.

"No, no. I have one in the closet."

"Pass the bread, please, Bianca." Maisie was hungry, but the only thing that appealed to her was Rudolpho's freshly baked ciabatta rolls. She was crampy and irritable and wanted to lie down.

The Braxton Hicks contractions had started a week ago. Her doctor had told her false labor late in the third trimester was common and nothing to worry about. Her uterus was just practicing for the main event.

Bianca passed the basket. "So, what do you think he'll look like?"

Maisie took a roll. "What do you mean by that?"

"Did you see pictures of the mother? Is she similar to you?"

"I am the mother! In every way that counts."

"Bianca!" Rudolpho snapped. "Basta! Enough."

Maisie couldn't get pregnant, so they'd used an egg donor. No one was supposed to know, but Beppe had accidentally let it slip. Bianca never missed an opportunity to rub Maisie's nose in it, especially by fawning over her own herd of naturally conceived children.

"Why are you like this?" Beppe asked his cousin.

Bianca didn't reply, but her smirk was all the comment she needed.

Maisie's fingernails dug into her palm. She'd completely crushed the roll. Dropping the mangled remains of the bread onto her plate, she struggled to her feet. "Excuse me. I'll be back in a minute."

She got up and started toward the half-bath. Pain nearly doubled her over, and a warm liquid rushed down her legs. Everyone at both the adult and children's tables gaped at her.

"I think my water just broke." *It's too early! Am I losing Joshua?* Her breath came fast and shallow as panic rattled her brain.

Maisie gazed down at the baby in her arms. She had thought the childbirth instructor had said all babies have slate-blue eyes at birth. His were tawny, like a lion's. Perhaps she'd remembered wrong. Both she and Beppe had brown eyes, so it didn't seem at all strange that their child would. Beppe sported a thick mane of wavy black hair, so that explained the wild shock of dark hair on Joshua's head.

"Best Christmas present ever!" Beppe leaned over and patted their son's back.

The door opened and Maisie expected it to be her father-in-law. Instead, it was an unfamiliar nurse leading three men dressed in black business suits that didn't quite fit.

The one closest beamed at them. "Good morning, Mr. and Mrs. Romano. We're from the Baby Care Division of Seven Hills Corporation. You have the most photogenic baby in the delivery room. We'd like to offer you a contract."

"Contract?" Beppe echoed.

"Yes, sir! To star in our advertising. Diapers, clothing, skin care—the whole shebang. One hundred thousand dollars for each year that he participates. Now, he'll probably age out around four. Although we do have a line of products for bed-wetting problems in older kids."

"We'll throw in a case of diaper rash cream," said another businessman.

"And a year's supply of diapers!" added the last one.

Maisie couldn't stop staring at the men as they talked. Their skin was as ill-fitting as their clothes, as if they wore makeup prosthetics that weren't fully attached and wobbled with each movement. Fear skittered over her arms and down her back like panicked spiders. She hugged Joshua closer.

Is this for some prank video? If it is, it's not funny. "Who let you people in here? I thought the maternity ward was more secure than this."

Beppe leaned back. "My wife... does have a point. It seems kind of weird for a bunch of corporate execs to be hanging out at a maternity ward on Christmas Day."

The businessmen looked at each other for a moment. The first one cleared his throat. "Well, we were alerted to the fact there is a very special baby here. When we saw his photo—"

"Someone sent you a picture of our baby?" Maisie's raised voice caused Joshua to cry. "See what you've done?" She began rocking him and humming.

Beppe got up, striding toward the men. The mystery nurse had apparently slipped out the door. "Leave. Now."

The first executive smiled. "That's a lot of money to turn down. I mean, how much *do* you have saved for little Joshua's college? Why don't you sleep on it and give us a call later?" He pressed a business card into Beppe's hand and the three of them left.

"I'm making a complaint to the hospital administration first thing tomorrow. Who do those people think they are?" Beppe stalked around the small room for some time before he finally settled down.

Maisie and Beppe had kept Joshua with them all afternoon. After dinner, she felt a rising dread at the idea of sending the baby back to the nursery for the night, especially after that same unknown nurse came in to check on them before the meal.

"Did you strap in the car seat base, Beppe?"

"I was going to do it in the morning. They aren't discharging you until tomorrow."

"I have a bad feeling about those men. We should leave tonight."

"Babe, you know your hormones are all over the place right now. You're over-reacting."

"But what if I'm not?"

"I don't think this is a good idea."

"It may not be. But that nurse. She's not on my care team. Why does she keep coming in my room? She was with those suits earlier."

Beppe shrugged. "That doesn't necessarily mean anything. Maybe your regular nurse had an emergency to deal with or something, and she was just filling in."

Maisie spoke just above a whisper, so as not to wake Joshua, but she wanted to scream. "Why don't you bel—"

Beppe followed her eyes to the bassinet where Joshua lay. The teddy bear that Rudolpho had bought danced in the air above the plastic bed.

"Who's… doing that?" Beppe's voice trembled. He got up and cautiously approached the bobbing bear. Arm outstretched like a blade, he ran it parallel to the toy: above…side… below… side… to form a box around the stuffed animal. "There's no wire."

"What if it's haunted?" Maisie had seen enough movies to know that any story that started with a haunted toy would not end well.

"No such thing as ghosts, Maise." He snatched the teddy from the air.

Joshua began to wail. A folded diaper from the stack on the counter flew up and smacked Beppe in the face.

"Ow!" He dropped the bear, which bobbed up and resumed its dance routine.

They both stared at the bassinet.

Maisie swallowed hard. "Do you think…?"

"A very special baby. That's what the man said."

Tears welled up in Maisie's eyes.

"I'll get the car. You pack your things."

Maisie had little to pack. She hadn't been expecting to deliver her baby during Christmas. No suitcase, but the hospital provided large plastic bags. She was grateful that Beppe had brought her some clothes to wear home after being discharged. She opted to leave the still-moist things from her arrival in the closet. She never really liked that blouse, anyway.

She tossed the diapers and a few small presents from Beppe's family into a plastic sack. Maisie stripped off the top sheet of her bed, then strapped Joshua into the baby carrier. Once he was secure, she wadded up the sheet and swaddled it in his blanket as if it was a baby, then carefully placed it in the bassinet.

She took a cushion from the visitor chair and put it and her pillow under the covers. If someone looked in from the door, they might not even notice that Maisie and Joshua were gone.

With a deep breath, Maisie picked up the bag and the baby and peered out the door. Two men in dark uniforms with no insignia walked past at the other end of her hallway, headed toward the nurse's station. She couldn't tell from this distance if they were police or military, but their presence triggered a surge of adrenaline. She had no way of knowing if they were connected to the strange businessmen from earlier, but she wasn't about to take any chances.

Grateful she was near the fire stairs, Maisie slipped out of her room and hurried to the exit.

"Hello?… Really? No, we didn't order any cable service—we're still out of town… Thanks for letting me know. I appreciate that, Mrs. Goodman. Hope you had a great Christmas. Happy New Year." Maisie disconnected the call.

The light changed and Beppe eased the car into motion. "What was that about?" he asked around a mouthful of hash browns from the drive through.

"Mrs. Goodman said that some men with a cable installation truck were in our house all day yesterday. Still think I was over-reacting?"

"Well…." He pulled over into a grocery store parking lot. "What do you think we should do?"

"They know we're here with your dad. I think we should withdraw as much cash as we can before we get too far away from here, then go someplace unexpected. Some random town where we don't have any ties and we can lie low while we try to figure out why those creepy men are so interested in Joshua." She looked into the rear-view mirror at the car seat in the back containing the sleeping baby. He was less than 30 hours old and was already nearly too big for the infant seat.

"I'm on vacation until the new year, and I guess I can start my paternity leave right after that. I'll have to call into the office, though."

"Do that before we get out of town. Then we should turn off our cell phones and get some pay-as-you-go ones."

They found a nearby discount store. Beppe put on a baseball cap and pulled the brim down to go inside and make his purchases. Maisie stayed in the car with Joshua and researched locations.

It wasn't long before Beppe returned and placed several stuffed shopping bags on the floor of the back seat.

Once he was buckled up, Maisie put down her phone. "Okay. How about Albuquerque?"

"New Mexico? I definitely don't know anybody there."

"That's the point. Albuquerque is a big enough city that nobody will notice three newcomers, and there are plenty of stores for whatever we need."

Beppe gripped the steering wheel. "Punch it into the navigator."

They found a motel that didn't ask any questions as long as they paid in cash. It wasn't especially clean or in a great part of town, but it was unlikely anyone would look for them there.

On the second evening of their stay, Maisie was giving Joshua a bath in his fancy new toddler tub. She kneeled on a folded towel next to the cracked hotel bathtub, with the green plastic tub placed inside. He could already sit up on his own, half a year ahead on this milestone, and he did so in the tub, playing with rubber bath toys.

Joshua had been restless and fussy all day. It seemed way too early for him to start teething, but then again, he could no longer fit into his infant car seat.

As Maisie wiped the soapy washcloth across Joshua's shoulder, it bumped over something rough. She dropped the cloth into the water and found a blister on the baby's back.

What happened here? She gently probed the area, and Joshua leaned into her hand. "Aww. Is that itchy?"

As she rubbed, a long strip of flesh peeled off. Her fingers brushed against hard, snakelike skin. She gasped and sat back on her haunches.

Joshua turned his head toward her. "Mama okay?"

The washcloth wrung itself out, then began scrubbing his ribs, revealing more colorful scales.

Judging by at least two coats of paint over the hinges, the door between the bathroom and bedroom had been missing for a long time. Out of the corner of her eye, she saw Beppe look up from the magazine he was reading and come running to the bathroom.

"Maise? What's hap—"

Beppe's jaw fell open when he caught sight of the pale teal and yellow striped scales where Joshua's soft baby skin should have been.

"What have we done?" Maisie whispered.

Her mind flashed back to the day they entered the Strieber Clinic. Her OB/GYN had referred them after a diagnosis of ovarian failure. She and Beppe had nowhere near enough money to pay for fertility treatments. But this clinic needed subjects for the final testing phase of their new procedure. Their *revolutionary* new procedure, as Dr. Strieber put it.

Maisie and Beppe would collect $10,000, plus testing and treatment, and maybe a baby. Dr. Strieber could get FDA approval for a technique that may give hope to thousands of couples without any. Signing a non-disclosure agreement under the circumstances hadn't seemed at all unreasonable.

"What's happening, Maise?" Beppe's voice trembled.

"Da! Da-da-da-daddy! Daddy want to play?"

"Joshua?" Maisie fought to keep her tone even. "How do you feel?" *How is he four days old and talking in complete sentences?*

"Hurts!" He grabbed his chest with both hands and pulled. The delicate baby skin stretched so much it made Maisie cringe. She wanted to vomit. To run away. She could do neither. Perforations began to appear below Joshua's belly button and along his ribs. The holes got bigger and bigger as he tugged. One by one, each hole ripped, cascading into an even larger one. He tore off his human covering, then threw it out of the tub.

Maisie covered her mouth with her hand to stifle her retching.

Beppe yelped as the tattered mess landed on his foot.

Joshua giggled. The glistening new scales on his throat, chest, and abdomen were the color of custard, and wider than those on his back and sides.

The discarded shoulder skin began to bubble and steam. In a very short time—perhaps a minute, but not more than two—it had boiled itself away to a powdery residue. Maisie pinched an edge of the torso flesh and tossed it into the tub as soon as it, too, started fizzing.

How is this happening? To my *baby?* A whimper escaped her lips as she dreaded what must surely come next.

Joshua opened his mouth wide and worked his jaw in circles, then pushed it out and brought it back in. The skin around his lips and eyes curled as it separated from what lay below it. Joshua tucked his thumbs under the torn flaps that dangled from his jaws and lifted. Everything except his thick black hair came off like a Halloween mask.

He dropped his former face on the smoking pile of flesh and grinned. "Mam. Ma!"

Maisie gazed into his golden eyes. He seemed to be the same sweet baby that she'd held in her arms, connected to her by an umbilical cord only a handful of days ago. The same one who'd cried at his first breath and fallen asleep on her chest, still damp from the womb.

His face wasn't *so* different. The scales were much finer than the others and hardly noticeable. Everything under the skin that had shed was basically the same shape as before, only the texture had changed. Even though her four-day-old baby was now the size of a three-year-old, he was still a child who needed love, comfort, and feeding. *Her* child.

Maisie rinsed the washcloth under the bathtub faucet and wiped down Joshua's new scaly exterior.

He giggled. "Tickles!"

"Let's get you dried off and into your jammies."

After stories were read, or rather, the one picture book they had was read many times, Joshua fell asleep. Maisie crept out of the bed and walked across the room to where Beppe sat in a chair, elbows on his knees and head in his hands.

He looked up as she got close. "What are we going to do, Maise? What is that thing?"

"That thing is your son," she hissed. "And we are *going* to take care of him."

His head drooped. "I wanted a baby. Not… this. If only you had been able—"

"Don't you dare blame this on me!" Maisie glanced over her shoulder to make sure she hadn't woken Joshua. "I was perfectly happy to adopt, but you insisted that the kid had to be your own flesh and blood. And here we are. We have to get him back to the clinic. Maybe the doctors know how to fix this. It could be a skin disorder that can be cleared up with medication. Like psoriasis or eczema."

"Maisie. Stop. He was eight pounds when he was born. Now he's closer to thirty-eight. That kid has quadrupled in size in only four days. That is not caused by psoriasis."

"Joshua is still our child."

"I think you're right about the clinic, though. Dr. Strieber has got to be told there's something wrong with his *revolutionary technique*."

Maisie and Beppe lay in the same bed, facing away from each other, as distant as possible. Beppe was a snorer, but all Maisie heard was quiet breathing. She couldn't sleep, either. It was all too much. She was far from recovered from childbirth, terrifying things were happening to their baby, and now she and Beppe couldn't even talk to each other.

A text notification chime stopped her from spiraling any further. They both sat up. Nobody should have this number. Nobody.

"Must be a friend of the former owner," Beppe whispered.

He's probably right. She stared at the blue display for what felt like hours. "I have to know for sure, though."

Maisie unlocked the phone and tapped the text app. "They're coming! Get out!"

Beppe read over her shoulder. He snatched the device from her hand and typed furiously. "Who is this? Who's coming?"

"A friend. Seven Hills Corp. They own Strieber Clinic. Go. Now."

They loaded their few belongings into their sedan, leaving Joshua for last. Beppe carried the sleeping tot out to the car and buckled him in as quietly as possible.

"I want to test something, Maise. How do we know that the texter was telling the truth?"

He drove to the gas station across the street. It was open 24 hours, and the pumps were brightly lit. Beppe pulled around to the side of the building, where it was mostly dark. They could observe the hotel and the bright lights in front of them would make it virtually impossible for them to be seen.

Maisie had just dozed off when Beppe elbowed her. Through bleary eyes, she watched a military-style assault vehicle pull into the parking lot and a dozen armed men in the same dark uniforms as the ones from the hospital pour out of it.

They made such quick work of the door that Maisie was sure they must have a key. Seconds after entering the room, they began to file out. The place was too small for all of them to have fit inside, anyway.

"How did they know where we were?" Maisie whispered.

"I don't know."

For twenty-eight long minutes, the men searched the area around the motel. One carried a plastic bag of white powder out of the room.

Maisie squinted. *Is that the skin residue from the bathtub?*

Once the running lights from the armored vehicle were out of sight, she finally breathed a sigh of relief. She turned to Beppe. "What now?"

He stared past her, out the window.

Chunk. Chunk. Chunk. Metal on glass.

Maisie swiveled her head. A man at her window held a handgun, pointing it at her ear. At least two other men stood a short distance behind him.

"Drive, Beppe, drive!"

He was frozen in fear.

The man tapped the window again. "Get out! This is our car now."

The gun flew out of his hand and started bashing him in the face. He groaned as blood spattered his clothes with each blow. The others scattered.

"No hurt Mama!" Joshua shouted from the back seat. "Bad! Bad! Bad!"

"Okay, baby. Joshua, stop. Please. That's enough."

Beppe thawed and hit the accelerator. The car screeched out of the darkness, nearly mowing down a man at a gas pump and missing sideswiping a car on the highway by inches.

"Thank you for saving us, Joshua. It was good that you helped, and you were right that he was a bad man. But please don't hurt people just because you are angry with them, okay?"

What if he decides he doesn't like something I've *told him to do?*

"Hungry! I am huuuungry." Joshua kicked his feet in an offhand way.

"Alright, baby. Hold on. We'll pull over in a minute and get you a snack."

Maisie's text chime sounded. It was a message from 'Unlisted,' the same as before. It consisted of a number with five digits after the decimal point, followed by a comma, then a similar number.

"What is it?" Beppe had finally slowed to something closer to the posted speed limit.

Maisie frowned at her phone. "Just numbers…" She held it up.

Beppe glanced at the device. "Those look like GPS coordinates. Put 'em into the navigator and let's see what they are."

As Maisie typed in the digits, she noticed a *crunch, crunch, crunch* coming from the back seat. The can of toddler puffs that had been in the diaper bag was now levitating near Joshua. *Well, that's one pit stop we don't have to make.*

The map came up on the screen, and the location pin showed a place in the mountains, about a hundred miles away. It looked very remote—Maisie couldn't even see a road to it.

"So, what do you think, Beppe?"

"I don't know. Is it a trap? Or a haven?"

"Good question. Whoever is on the other end did warn us to leave, though."

They drove in silence for a few minutes.

"In half a mile, turn left onto Barney Road," the navigator urged.

"Turn left! Left!" Joshua giggled from the back seat.

Beppe turned left.

They had to park the car on the shoulder and hike up into the low mountains. Joshua was walking, but not well, so Beppe carried him. Maisie hauled the diaper bag, a backpack with what little food and water they had, and the phone with the GPS coordinates.

"Ow!" Maisie rubbed her arm, smearing blood across it. A bare, thorny branch had snagged her and dug a shallow red trench down her arm.

"I'm ready for a break, anyway. Let's sit down for a minute. Do you need a bandage?" Beppe set Joshua down on a flat rock.

"No, it's just a scratch."

Joshua crawled down from his perch and toddled to his mother. Thinking he wanted a cuddle, Maisie stretched her arms out to him. He grabbed her wrist as if for balance, then began licking the blood off her arm.

"Joshua! What are you doing? Stop that!" Maisie recoiled.

For the first time, the tawny eyes that looked back at her did not seem like those of a child.

"Honey, let's not do that, okay?"

He kept eye contact with her as his long, narrow tongue lapped up the last trickle of red.

Beppe pressed both hands against the sides of his head and interlaced his fingers over the top.

Joshua turned to follow his father's gaze at the creek gurgling nearby. "Daddy, what does 'drown' mean?"

Color drained from Beppe's face. "N-nothing. Don't worry about it."

They resumed their hike, and after another hour, they came to an opening in the side of a cliff.

"This seems to be it." Maisie peered into the cave mouth without getting any closer.

"Hello!"

The two parents jumped at the sound of the man's voice. Joshua did not.

"Welcome Maisie and Beppe. I am Sobek. I have been sending the texts to guide you away from those soldiers."

He was dressed in desert camo military fatigues, but his face had the same finely textured scales as Joshua's, only they were sand colored, almost golden. His nose and mouth protruded into a little more of a snout, but he looked mostly human.

"Um. Hi." Beppe switched Joshua to his other hip.

Maisie took a step closer to her son. "How do you know our names?"

"Won't you come inside? Those soldiers who've been following you for the past ten miles will be along soon."

The family hurried into the cave. Countless pairs of golden eyes glowed in the late afternoon rays of sun that sliced through the stony entrance.

"Oh! There are so many children here." *Where are their parents?*

Sobek brushed his hand across the wall, and something slid down, a door of sorts. Maisie could see through it, as if it was tinted glass.

A half-dozen soldiers in dark uniforms appeared. Maisie reasoned that the door must look like rock to them, because they didn't appear to note it in any way as they passed.

Sobek shook his head. "They would claim they are out to rescue you. But *they* want to take your baby away and experiment on him. *We* want to help him grow up strong and free."

"Glad to hear it." Beppe nodded.

Joshua wriggled and kicked. "Down!"

Beppe placed him gently on the ground. He scurried to the other children.

Sobek grinned. "You could have just signed the contract on the day of his birth. It would have been easier for you. But it is good for us that you have arrived. We donated eggs to *you*. Now you can make a donation to *us*."

"I don't have any cash." Beppe patted the wallet in his pocket.

Sobek laughed. "We don't use that here. No, the donation we require is blood."

"Blood!" Maisie shuddered at the memory of Joshua licking her wound.

"H-how much do you need?" Beppe stammered.

Sobek's wide smile displayed rows of sharp teeth. "All of it."

A String of Lights
By A. B. Richards

THE mail truck had just pulled away, and I slipped on my shoes.

It was a little colder than I expected, but walking to the end of the driveway and back wouldn't kill me. The smell of wood smoke drifting from nearby chimneys sparked happy holiday memories as I opened the mailbox. Bill. Junk. Junk. Unknown. Bill. Junk. No credit card. *When is that damn replacement going to get here?*

"Hey, Annette! How are things?"

I looked up from my mail to see my across-the-street neighbor, Harlan, waving at me.

He and his wife were the nicest people. "Taking a break from putting up those decorations?" His Christmas extravaganza always attracted crowds. It was even on the local news once.

"Yeah. I'll have to wait for my son-in-law to come tomorrow to help get Santa and the sleigh up on the roof, but I can at least get some of the lights done."

I shivered and hugged myself. "With that twelve-foot tinsel tree and the mini railroad going on underneath it, people probably won't notice the lights."

He threw his head back and laughed, the kind of deep belly laugh that shook his entire body. "They'd better! I paid extra for these faceted globe ones. Besides, we still have more to go. I added a motion-activated snowman this year. Ryan's bringing it tomorrow." He cocked his head. "You must be freezing. Don't let me keep you."

"Alright. See you later." I raised my handful of mail in a half-wave.

I scurried into my warm house and poured more hot water from the kettle into my teacup. My unfinished stack of Christmas cards awaited. I was trying to be better about sending them out this year. Twilight deepened as I sat on the couch and looked out the window, hoping the sparkling spectacle of Harlan's decorations would get me in the mood.

Raul, Harlan's next-door neighbor to the north, had stopped by for a chat. The two men appeared to be having an amicable visit, even laughing together, as Harlan stood there with a blinking string of lights in his hands. A sense of gratitude washed over me—I was lucky to live in a safe neighborhood where folks knew each other. There was a real feeling of community here. Made writing my cards that much easier.

When I looked up again, my mind struggled to process what I was seeing. My eyes passed along a message, and my brain flat out rejected it.

Little round Christmas lights blinked cheerfully under Raul's jaw as he frantically tried to pull them away. Harlan had wrapped the string of lights around his friend's throat and was pulling them tight.

Raul's face was pure terror. Harlan's was nonchalant. This could not be happening.

And yet it was.

I sat there frozen, not knowing what to do. Was this a prank? Will they get mad if I call 9-1-1? All indications were that Harlan was murdering Raul, but I simply couldn't bring myself to believe it.

Maybe Raul said something, and Harlan took it the wrong way? I'd go out there and ask what was going on. This was not a dangerous neighborhood. There was a behavior code. If it was a joke or a misunderstanding, my interruption would put a stop to it. Break it up and they'd talk it out later. That's how we did things here. And if it was a prank, we'd all have a laugh.

Phone in hand, just in case, I opened the front door and hurried about half-way down my walkway. "Hey, Harlan! What's going on there?"

He did not release Raul, who was sinking to his knees. Slowly, Harlan's head turned toward me, and a bone-chilling smile crept over his face. He dropped the string of lights and Raul collapsed on the sidewalk.

Without breaking eye contact, Harlan reached to the side of his tool belt and pulled out a claw hammer. He raised it high and began striding in my direction.

It took a moment for my brain to register the danger. I turned and fled, slamming the door and turning the deadbolt just as Harlan started pounding on the wood.

I raised my hand to dial 9-1-1, but my phone was gone. *Shit.* I must have dropped it when I started running. My parents were the only people I knew who still had a landline. And I wished desperately for one now.

He could easily break through the picture window in the living room. I only had a few seconds to decide what to do next.

What is it they tell you?

Run.

Hide.

Fight.

Car's in the driveway, can't get to it.

He knows I'm in here.

Fight? Can't win.

The front door cracked and splintered.

Out of time.

I bolted out the back door. I'd go around the side while he was in the house. It wouldn't take him long to figure out what I'd done, so it would only buy me a minute—two if I was lucky.

Tears streamed down my face as I struggled with the latch. I had to put my foot under the gate and lift to get the bar of the latch free, but my hands were shaking so hard I could barely work the closure.

Is this how I die?

Finally, the gate swung open. I made sure to slam it shut so Harlan would have to deal with the same problem.

Across the street, Raul was on all fours on the sidewalk, the colored string of lights blinking gaily on the dead grass in Harlan's yard.

I sprinted to Raul. "Get up! Get up! He's coming!"

I grabbed his hand and pulled as hard as I could. With his arm slung over my shoulder, we stumbled to his house and squeezed through the front door together.

"What on Earth…?" Sheila—his wife—came out of the kitchen, drying a skillet with a dish towel.

"Call 9-1-1! He needs an ambulance!"

I twisted the knob on the deadbolt and looked out through the peephole. Harlan jogged out through my side gate and stood in the driveway. His head slowly rotated from south to north, and his gaze stopped at Raul's front door.

With a malicious grin, he raised the hammer and began to smash up my car. I couldn't bear to watch, so I turned toward Raul and Sheila.

She held her phone to her ear and relayed information from her husband to someone at the other end of the call.

Surely help was on the way. My legs got wobbly, so I leaned against the smooth steel door and slid down to the floor. I drew my knees up to my chest and sobbed.

Time seemed to shrink and stretch randomly, so I don't know how long it took before red and blue lights strobed through the front windows. When the knock came at the front door, I crawled out of the way, not trusting my legs to support my weight.

Paramedics with a stretcher hustled in, followed by a couple of police officers. The EMTs measured Raul's vital signs, and he answered their questions in a raspy voice. I could not stop staring at the angry red marks around his throat that would surely turn into black and purple bruises.

One of the officers kneeled beside me. "Annette?"

I finally tore my eyes away from Raul and looked into the kneeling man's face and nodded.

"Would you like to sit here? It might be more comfortable."

He stood and pulled out two chairs at the nearby dining table. I got to my feet. My whole body felt like Jello in an earthquake, but I made my way across the room without falling and sat in one of Sheila's fancy dining chairs.

The officer retrieved a small notebook from the depths of his bullet-proof vest.

"Annette, tell me what happened."

I just looked at him and blinked. I seemed to have forgotten how to make the words in my brain come out of my mouth.

The crack of a gunshot shattered the quiet, and I jumped. The second officer stepped outside to investigate. Raul, now in a neck brace, was being strapped onto the stretcher in preparation for transport.

The second officer returned and spoke with the EMTs. He held the door open while they wheeled Raul out, Sheila close behind them. After the gurney cleared the doorway, he came over to speak quietly to the officer at the table. His back was to me, and I couldn't hear most of what he said, but I made out the words, 'didn't get him' and 'K-9 unit.'

He moved closer to the door and began texting on his phone.

"Alright, Annette. Sorry for the interruption. Let's start again. What happened this evening?"

After a few stammering starts, I finally found my voice. Once moving, the story spewed out like vomit, leaving the bitter taste of bile in my mouth.

"Do you have someplace you can stay tonight, ma'am?"

"My-my parents' place. But I lost my phone."

"I'll call them for you."

I wrote down the number.

I sat in my parents' living room, talking on the phone. I finally found a real estate agent who was willing to look at my house before Christmas. The crime scene tape had come down and the remains of my car had been towed away. A new front door was being installed even as we spoke.

I admit to being a little cagey when she asked why I wanted to sell, and she seemed suspicious.

"Has anyone died in the house? We do have to report that."

"No. No one died there." *I almost did, but that didn't count, did it?* "As I said, I need to be closer to my parents." That wasn't a lie, although I may not have mentioned why it was so.

We made an appointment for a walkthrough tomorrow, when my dad started his Christmas vacation and could go with me.

Harlan was still on the loose, after all.

From what the detectives told me, Raul had no idea what had caused Harlan to snap. One minute they were talking about holiday lights, the next he was being strangled. Harlan's wife hadn't noticed any odd behavior leading up to the incident. Afterward, she'd unplugged all the decorations and gone to Wisconsin to spend the holidays with her sister. She may or may not return.

I helped Mom cook dinner and Dad tidied up the kitchen while we girls wrapped Christmas presents for my siblings. The aroma of fresh-baked bread lingered in the dining room, making me crave another slice, even though I was stuffed to the gills.

It was strange, I'll admit, being back in my parents' house in my thirties. But it was a sanctuary. I was nurtured and protected here.

When Dad came into the living room, he turned on the TV and we watched the end of yet one more variation of *A Christmas Carol.* I suppose it was tradition—he'd been watching that movie, or riffs on it, for as long as I could remember. I almost felt like a kid getting ready for a visit from Santa as I brushed my teeth.

At first, I wasn't sure what woke me.

Tap. Tap. Tap.

The noise came from the window. Glowing red, green, blue, and yellow danced on the windowsill, muted and blurred by the cotton drapery. Curious, I got out of bed and tiptoed over to the light show. *Had the neighbors put up lights after I went to bed?* I pulled back the curtain.

Strung haphazardly across my window and cheerfully blinking in the dark, was a string of lights. Faceted globe Christmas lights.

Delivery
By A. B. Richards

I FINALLY got a job. At least for a few months. Never thought I'd be delivering packages for a living, but here we are.

I actually like the trips that are just out of town. Less traffic, more scenery. Downside is more time to think. If I think too much about my precarious position in this world, I just get depressed. Maybe my next lottery ticket would hit, and it would be a merry Christmas, after all.

Anyway, I found myself bumping down a gravel road late in the afternoon. I had to double-check the address—the house looked like it had been abandoned for years, if not decades—but they matched. I drove down the short driveway, which was really just two worn tracks through the overgrown yard to the dilapidated garage.

I put my van in park and picked up the box. It was wrapped in glossy, dark crimson paper with a forest green bow. The tag read, "To Santa Claws, From: Margaret." I chuckled at the misspelling. And don't presents come *from* Santa Claus?

Anyway, I walked up the rickety steps, dodging a hole in the porch. Something underneath skittered away as I approached. A handwritten, weather-stained note was taped to the door with discolored cellophane tape.

Leave deliveries in back yard
Please
Thank you

I didn't really like the idea of going to the back of someone's house, where I couldn't be seen from the road. Where someone might be lying in wait. But it was also easy to believe this front door might be permanently stuck.

With a sigh, I took the pepper spray out of my pocket and held it at the ready. I always carry it, because, while I am an animal lover, I also don't want to get bitten by people's loose dogs.

"Hello?" I called as I walked slowly around the corner. "Anyone back here?" Not that I thought any bad guys planning to ambush me would answer, but if the homeowner was out in the yard, I didn't want to frighten them.

At the gate I stopped dead—not literally, but almost. The front of the house looked like it was about to fall down. The back was surrounded by a crisp white picket fence. A marble fountain gurgled from a slate rectangle in the center of the manicured lawn. The covered porch had rocking chairs and looked recently painted.

Even weirder than that, though, were the presents. I counted six—all boxes of identical size to the one I carried. All dressed in somber holiday paper and bows. The gate creaked as I opened it, a blast of chilly air rushed over me.

"Hello?"

No one responded to my call this time either. Well, when in Rome....

I set the box down next to another, which was also addressed to "Santa Claws," but this one was from "Timothy."

Fumbling with the reader, I scanned the barcode and took a picture as proof of delivery. Glad to be rid of this package, movement caught my eye as I turned toward the gate. I glanced up at the windows and was sure I saw a figure with antlers looking out the glass. By the time I half-jogged to my car, I had convinced myself it was just a reflection of the huge old oak tree in the yard. Even as I laughed about it, I backed out of the driveway as fast as I could, suddenly eager to get back to the city.

I was in the storefront two days later, picking up my next round of deliveries. A middle-aged woman in a purple and white knit hat and matching puffy jacket rushed through the door, tears streaking her makeup.

"Please!" she said. "Please, you have to help me."

Cindy held up a hand from behind the cash register. "Are you having a medical emergency?"

The woman shook her head.

"Okay. If you're not in physical danger, it'll be just a minute, ma'am. As soon as I'm done with this customer, I'll help you."

Whimpering and sniffling, she stood a few feet behind the man filling out a form at the register. When he was finally done, she all but thrust herself at the counter.

"How may I help you?" Cindy plastered on her best counter-help face.

"Two days ago," she panted. "I brought a package in for delivery. I need it back."

Cindy shook her head. "I'm sorry. The package has already been delivered. There's nothing we can do about it. Can't you contact the person you sent it to?"

"No… no… no," she choked out between sobs. "The shipping label was given to me in a sealed envelope. Please. I have to have it back. My name is Margaret Springer. You have to have a record of where it went."

"Of course we do. But I can't just give that out to any random person who walks through my door."

"Please...." Margaret dissolved into sobs.

"I wish I could help you. Really, I do. It's out of my hands. I'm going to have to ask you to step aside so I can help the next customer."

Margaret's shoulders slumped and she trudged toward the door. Cindy hadn't been out to that freaky place. *I* had. Feeling sorry for the woman, I followed her. When we were outside, I jogged up even with her.

"Ma'am? Excuse me. I couldn't help overhearing. I delivered a package from a Margaret two days ago. If you can describe what it looked like, I'll tell you where I took it."

She grabbed me in a hug, nearly squeezing the breath out of me. "Thank you! Thank you!" Margaret let go to blot her eyes with a soggy tissue. "It had dark red paper, shiny, dark green bow. Addressed to 'Santa Claws,' that's c-l-a-w-s."

"That's the package I delivered. Let's go to your car." I gave her the general directions on the way.

When she unlocked her door, I asked if she had a piece of paper. She handed me a faded receipt, and I wrote down the address. I had committed it to memory, in case I had to take other packages out there.

"Thank you again!"

"Sure. Hope you find what you're looking for."

The next day, two police officers walked into the store. They talked to Cindy as I scanned packages into my custody. I didn't

127

pay much attention, until I heard the name Margaret Springer. Apparently, she was missing.

Shit. Should I have kept the address to myself? Did I send her to her doom?

I tilted the dolly and wheeled the packages out to my van, keeping an eye on the door. When the officers came out, I approached them.

"Excuse me. I might be able to help." I told them what had happened yesterday and gave them the address of the creepy old house with the backyard full of gifts. I tried showing them the picture of the delivered package, but it was completely black. Perhaps I'd screwed up, but all the other photos came out just fine. The officers thanked me and left. Maybe *they* could sort all that stuff out.

I stopped for gas and a lotto ticket Saturday on my way to pick up my deliveries, I was horrified to find two more 'Santa Claws' packages. I thought about quitting my job then and there, but, since my rent wasn't going to pay itself, I called my cousin Ty instead. I knew he'd be home because he had a severe allergy to gainful employment, and only had friends when he had money. His place was close to my planned route, so it wouldn't be more than ten minutes out of my way.

I told him all about my first trip out there. He laughed at me.

"Are you trying to prank me? Has somebody put you up to delivering me to a surprise birthday party?"

It's a surprise to me, too. Hadn't realized it was his birthday today. "No. I get that you don't believe me. *I* wouldn't have believed me, if I hadn't been there myself."

"Okay. Whatever you say."

It wasn't worth my breath to try convincing him. He'd see it up close and personal when we got there. We talked about things the rest of the way.

I was down to the last two boxes, and cold dread twisted my innards. "Alright, Ty. Here we go. Get ready to be weirded out."

"Sure thing." A suppressed smile crinkled the corners of his mouth.

It was even later in the afternoon than my first trip. The winter dark was nipping at our heels, and I drove as fast as I felt I could without sliding all over the gravel. We pulled up in what passed for a driveway, Ty looking around suspiciously. He must have really expected that surprise birthday party.

I let him carry the heavier package. It was a semi-matte green that made me think of algae. The gate creaked as we passed through. A few more presents had arrived. I looked for Margaret's, but it was gone. I hoped that was a good thing.

While I scanned the barcodes and took the photos, Ty snooped around the yard.

A purple and white knit hat lay at the foot of the tree that Ty stood next to. I slipped my phone into my pocket. "Dude! Come back here. Let's go already."

"Is this it? Shouldn't we hang around a minute?"

I expect that Margaret Singer hung around a minute too long.

The oak tree behind him shuddered and burst open. A tall thing—I don't know what to call it—stepped out. It wasn't exactly human, but it wasn't entirely animal, either. The creature's ragged clothes were a blotchy red, as if stained by splashes and drops rather than dyed in a vat. The head... I may or may not have wet myself. Its face was the skull of some carnivore—a wolf, or perhaps a bear? And it had antlers. Deer antlers.

Taller than Ty—and he was a solid six foot—it reached out with a too-long arm and wrapped its bony clawed hand around his neck as he started to flee.

"Well," the thing said, its voice like stone sliding over gravel. "It seems you have brought me a present."

Ty gasped and gurgled as he pulled at what passed for fingers gripping his throat.

"N-n-o. Let him go!"

With a velociraptor shaped claw, the monster cut a gash down Ty's arm and then licked his blood from it. I don't know how it was possible for it to smile with no skin and no lips, but I'm sure that it did. Ty's feet kicked wildly as it lifted him off the ground.

"Choose. This offering for a wish. Or you offer yourself as a penalty for your trespass."

So, I could let that thing kill me, or I could sacrifice my ne'er-do-well cousin and get a wish? I cleared my throat. "What kind of wish?"

Ty squeaked and struggled harder.

The monstrous creature shook him. "The kind you wish for every Saturday."

"You can make me win the lotto?"

"I can make many things happen."

I closed my eyes and sucked in a deep breath. "I'm so sorry, Ty."

I'm not sure what happened next. It seems like I just blinked and I was on the highway headed back to town. On the off chance that anyone noticed Ty was missing, I thought about a cover story.

Last Christmas was the best one ever. I was able to fix up my parents' house and buy my sister a brand-new car.

I didn't want to go crazy and buy some giant mansion and then go broke paying the taxes on the thing. I bought a nice house out in the country. It wasn't too big but was two stories and had a wrap-around verandah. The backyard was my de-stress oasis. I planted the tallest red oak tree I could find in the back corner and put up a big marble fountain. The birds loved it. I enjoyed it almost as much as they did, listening to it gurgle and splash while I sat on the porch in my rocking chair having a glass of wine and reading a book.

Sometimes I wonder what exactly happened to Ty, but he was a lost cause long before I ever delivered a box to that abandoned house.

For the first time, I hosted Thanksgiving at my house. It was a hit and I looked forward to many more.

On Friday morning, I saw someone in my backyard.

"What the hell?"

I pulled on my bathrobe, ran downstairs, and yanked open the French doors.

No one was in the yard.

But there was a wrapped present. The tag read, "To Santa Claws, From Cindy."

Away in a Manger

By Holley Dey

"YOU'RE a lifesaver, Amity!" Valerie climbed down from the stepladder.

"That's what friends are for, right?" Amity folded the ladder and pulled her jacket tighter around her neck. The sun, small against the denim blue sky, seemed too far away to offer much warmth.

"This isn't quite how I planned to spend my Saturday morning." Amity surveyed the unfamiliar backyard.

"I know. I really appreciate you giving me a ride this morning." Valerie took the ladder from her friend. "Don't you usually go riding on the weekends?"

"I'll go later, when it warms up a bit."

Valerie raised the stepladder. "I'll go put this back in the shed."

She took in the elegant oasis. Water bubbled over glistening rocks before tumbling into the kidney-shaped pool. The outdoor kitchen under the covered patio was fancier than the indoor kitchen at her home. She was admiring the stone raised beds when Valerie trotted up behind her and grabbed her arm with a trembling hand.

"Let's go. Now."

"What's the—" Amity cut herself off when she caught sight of Valerie's ashen face. She hurried out the back gate with her friend.

They got into Amity's SUV and she started the engine. "Valerie? What happened?"

"There's a body in the shed."

"A *what?*"

"A man. A man in a beige sweater is dead in there."

The vehicle lurched away from the curb as Amity tapped the gas, then slammed on the brake to avoid a passing truck. "Let's just go to the police station."

The door to the interrogation room opened and a stern woman walked in with a notebook.

"Afternoon. I'm Detective Farmer. The desk sergeant said you found a body?"

"Y-yes, ma'am." Valerie hugged herself. "I'm a landscape designer. We were at a client's house working on installing Christmas lights. My friend Amity was helping me."

Detective Farmer scrutinized Amity's face. "Have we met? It's Hudson, right? From the stable incident last year?"

Amity shifted uncomfortably. "Yes, ma'am"

"Did you also see the body?"

"No."

The detective took their contact information, then turned back to Valerie. "Alright. Tell me what happened."

"My car's in the shop. I had to go to a Christmas light install at a client's house and Amity drove me. I was taking pictures so I could draft the design, and I needed some elevation. After a little searching, I found a stepladder in the shed in the backyard. I noticed a blue plastic tarp spread over something in the corner, but didn't think much about it. Only when I put the ladder back, I accidentally caught the edge of the tarp with the metal foot and pulled it away. And there he was."

"Tell me about him. How did you know he was dead?"

"Well… he didn't move when I pulled the tarp off him. I even said 'sorry' out of reflex. His eyes were open, staring at the wall. And he looked kinda… greenish. For a second, I thought it was my Uncle Harry. But he would never wear a beige sweater."

"Alright. What does your Uncle Harry look like?"

"He's middle-aged. Hair was mostly black but had some grey. Thick black mustache. Did I mention he had a beige sweater?"

"Yes, you did." Detective Farmer nodded as she jotted notes. "Anything else?"

Valerie shook her head. "That's all I remember."

"Did you touch anything?"

"No! I dropped the ladder and ran."

"What was the name of the client?"

"Dorothy Whittington."

The detective took down Mrs. Whittington's address and phone number. "Okay. Thanks for letting us know. We'll look into it."

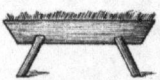

Bunny's Coffee and More had the best house-made pastries on this side of town. Amity wished they would sell candles with the coffee and spice aroma that filled the shop. She and Valerie had mostly finished their drinks when Valerie's phone rang.

"Mrs. Whittington?"

The caller's voice was so loud that Amity could hear the conversation clearly.

"How dare you call the police to my residence!"

"There was a body in the shed. What was I supposed to do?"

"Body! There is not and never was a body in my shed. Are you on drugs? That might make you hallucinate bodies in sheds."

"I didn't hallucinate anything, ma'am. There was a man—"

"The police didn't find any man, and now all the neighbors are standing out in their yards to see why three police cars with flashing lights are in front of my house!"

"What do you mean, they didn't find a body?"

"Is this a prank? A joke? Did someone put you up to this?"

"No! I—"

"Don't come back here. Your services are no longer required. And I will review your business accordingly."

Valerie put her elbows on the table and rested her forehead on her palms. Without looking up, she shook her head. "I'm not crazy."

"Of course you aren't. I believe you. Maybe… maybe it was just a hyper-realistic Halloween decoration?"

"If that was true, she would have said something like, 'Oh, dear. You stumbled across one of our hyper-realistic Halloween decorations. So sorry to frighten you.' And she wouldn't have fired me and threatened bad reviews."

"There's that."

Valerie sighed and looked up. "She was my first Christmas lights customer. Now, probably my last. Don't know what I'm gonna do. Landscape design customers are almost non-existent in the winter. And now if she goes around giving me nasty reviews…"

Valerie's phone rang again. She picked it up and muttered under her breath. This caller was soft-spoken, and Amity couldn't hear what was said.

"Hello?… This is she… I understand that. But there really was a body!… I have no idea… of course not!… yes, ma'am." Valerie turned off her phone.

"Who was that?"

"Detective Farmer, calling to advise me that filing a false police report is a Class B misdemeanor with a $2,000 fine, should she choose to pursue it."

"Ouch." Amity peered hopefully into the bottom of her empty cup. "You wanna go out to the barn with me? It may take your mind off things."

"Sure. Not like I've got anything else to do."

Sunday morning's sun wasn't even up yet. Amber stood next to the bed by Amity's head and groaned. The black and tan shepherd mix was normally the silent partner of Amity's pair of dogs. Except when meals were late. She definitely had opinions about that.

Amity tried to roll over, but eighty pounds of brindle and white dog blocked her way. Jax uncurled himself and took a leisurely stretch before jumping off the bed with a loud fart.

"Ugg." Amity's nose wrinkled. "What did you eat?"

He pricked his ears and wagged his tail, staring at her with one blue eye and one brown.

There was no going back to sleep now. She hurried out of bed to escape the fumes. There would be fresh air in the kitchen. Where the dog food was kept.

With a quick check to make sure there were no critters in the backyard, she turned the dogs out while she made their breakfast.

After the three of them had eaten, Amity put a sweater on smooth-haired Jax and grabbed her heavy jacket. They'd take a long stroll around the town square and check out the holiday decorations. She'd seen a truck unloading items in front of the Methodist church for their nativity scene on her way home from work on Friday. Crews with cherry pickers were hanging red and gold tinsel bows on streetlights downtown when Amity had picked up Valerie yesterday.

As she turned the corner, she was surprised to see the huge crowd at the Methodist church. And even more surprised to see yellow crime scene tape and flashing lights. As she got closer, Detective Farmer rose from a kneeling position and began speaking to a well-dressed gentleman. Amity recognized Detective Myles from the stable incident.

Detective Farmer glanced her way, then did a double take. She said something to a uniformed officer, who ducked under the yellow tape and began striding toward Amity. This did not go unnoticed by Jax and Amber, who stopped and perked up their ears.

The officer stopped about ten feet in front of Amity and the dogs. "Detective Farmer wants to talk to you."

"Right now? I have the dogs…."

"Yes, ma'am. You can tie them to the bicycle rack over there."

Amity swallowed and did as she was asked. She followed the officer underneath the yellow tape to Detective Farmer.

"I don't understand. Why do you need—"

Her eyes fell on the nativity. A man sprawled in the manger on top of Baby Jesus. A man with a thick black mustache and a beige sweater.

Amity gasped. "Valerie was right!" She swallowed hard and looked away. It seemed disrespectful to gawp at the poor corpse.

"About Valerie." Detective Farmer peeled off her blue nitrile gloves. "Do you know where we can find her?"

"She's not at home?"

"We wouldn't be asking if she were, Miss Hudson. Or if she would answer her phone."

"She hadn't m-mentioned any travel plans that I remember."

"If you hear from her, tell her to call me. You still have my card?"

"Yes."

Amity wanted nothing more than to get away from the investigation and the dead man. "Can I go?"

"Yes. I'll call you if I need you."

Detective Myles raised the yellow tape for her, and Amity was surprised when he also ducked under it.

"Those your dogs?" He gestured toward Jax and Amber.

"Yeah." Amity filled in the awkward silence with, "I got them from a rescue. The brindle is Jax, and the black and tan one is Amber."

"You still have your horse?"

Surprised he remembered, Amity stopped walking. "Of course." *Was he really just being nice, or did he have an ulterior motive?* "Are you the good cop?"

Detecitve Myles chuckled. "Perhaps. I know that Farmer can come off as abrasive sometimes. But she's really good at her job. My approach is a little different, but we have the same goal." He reached into his pocket and pulled out a metal business card case. "If you remember anything else, give me a call."

"I'll do that." Amity took the card and put it in the small crossbody bag that contained her keys, her phone, and a roll of dog poop bags.

She had run each leash through the loop handle around the bar of the bike rack and then re-clipped it to the corresponding collar. The moment she unclipped Amber's leash to get it off the bar, the dog broke free and lunged at Detective Myles.

Amity gasped in horror.

Seemingly in slow motion, his hands rose to protect his face as the dog jumped up.

She licked his chin, his hands, and his ear in that one leap. Amber stood on her hind legs, tail raising a gale force wind, trying to lick his face.

"I'm so sorry. Amber never does that!" Amity snapped the leash on the dog's collar and pulled her away.

"It's okay. When I was a kid, my mom had a dog that looked very similar. I still miss that dog sometimes." He leaned over and scratched Amber behind the ears. "She looks so much like Paula, she could be her re-incarnation."

A blue norther had blown in quicker than Amity had estimated and soaked her and her horse with cold rain and sleet while they were on a trail ride around the cross-country field. She'd dried off Destiny as best she could, then blanketed the shivering mare. Then she helped her trainer—Jackie—make warm bran mashes for all the horses and blanket them.

Amity had just pulled out of the barn driveway when her phone rang. She tapped the infotainment display. "Valerie! Where have you been? I tried calling you all morning."

"Girl. I dropped my cell into the koi pond and had to go get a new one. Between the carrier's Christmas deals and people shopping for new gadgets, it took hours to get the dumb thing replaced. And then the Uber driver got lost on the way to pick me up. What's going on?"

"You didn't hear?"

"Hear what? I just got home."

"Mr. Beige Sweater turned up in the manger at the Methodist church's nativity scene this morning."

"What!"

"Looks like you were right. You should have seen the look on that detective's face when I pointed that out."

"Wait… you were there? Also, are you out blowing leaves?"

"No. Just the heat on high in the car. So, this morning I had taken the dogs out for a walk and planned to look at the Christmas decorations around town, but I didn't get very far before I ran into the crime scene. Detective Farmer was looking for you. You should probably call her as soon as possible."

"Ugh. That woman is terrifying."

"All the more reason to stay on her good side."

Amity listened to the radio while she cooked dinner. According to the local news, Mr. Beige Sweater was actually called Frank Harmon. He was semi-retired and a volunteer at the Methodist church. His family had set up a Go Fund Me for his funeral expenses. While her bread was baking, she made a contribution.

"Have you done the load testing yet?" Amity asked Rod, her coworker from the testing group.

"Not yet. There's a bug in one of the procedure calls that you guys have to fix before we can do that."

"Okay. I'll get Sanjay on it. Thanks."

Amity mostly enjoyed her job as a software engineer, but some days she felt like a fireman, rushing to put out fires all over the place. It was only Wednesday, but the week already seemed like it had gone on for eight days.

Within two breaths of hanging up with Rod, her phone rang again. "Amity Hudson."

"Amity? It's Phyllis."

Why was Valerie's mother calling her, and in the middle of the day? "Oh, hey. What's going on?"

"Have you heard from Val today? I was supposed to pick her up this morning to get her car, but she wasn't home and she's not answering her phone. I just talked to her last night."

"No, I haven't. Maybe she lost her phone again? Or she was in a rush and got an Uber to the car shop?"

"It's not like her to make plans with me, then go off and do something else. She has a couple of appointments this afternoon, so she was pretty desperate to get her car, though."

"Well, could be the car was ready earlier than promised, and she didn't want to bother you. I'm sure she'll give you a call soon."

"I hope you're right."

On her way home from work, Amity called Valerie. It rolled straight to voice mail. Must be turned off while she was talking to a client.

She called Valerie again before she went to bed with the same result.

Amity left early for work and stopped by the police station. She had no idea what time detectives showed up for work, but if Detective Myles wasn't there, she could at least leave him a note.

She gave her name to the desk sergeant, and she made a call. "Detective Myles will be with you in a moment."

It was a lot more than a moment, and Amity would be late for work if she waited much longer. The elevator dinged and out stepped a uniformed officer.

"Detective Myles can see you now."

Amity hesitated, but since she was already here…. "Thank you."

They rode in silence to the fifth floor. The officer led her through a maze of cubicles until they reached one in the far corner.

Detective Myles stood and reached out his hand. "Good morning, Amity. Thanks for coming by. What do you have for me?"

She shook his hand. It was much warmer than she'd expected. He gestured to a chair in front of his desk and she sat down.

"Valerie is missing again."

"Oh?"

"Yeah. Her mom called me yesterday, saying she was supposed to take Valerie to pick up her car, but she was a no-show. I called her a couple of times and it went straight to voice mail."

Detective Myles looked through some notes. "Yes. Phyllis did call yesterday afternoon and spoke with Detective Farmer. Then she came in and filed a missing person report."

Amity wasn't sure whether to feel relief that the police were working on it or irritable that the detective would string her along and pretend not to know. *Guess in his line of work, everyone's a suspect.* "I'm worried about her. Just wanted to make sure you were on it." Her eyes fell on a piece of paper with a long string of random letters and numbers lying on Myles' desk. "Huh. I wouldn't have pegged you as a crypto guy."

"A what?"

"Cryptocurrency. Is that your wallet?"

"Not mine. It was on a scrap of paper in Mr. Harmon's pocket. I'd planned to ask the tech guys if they thought it was some kind of password, but a crypto wallet makes perfect sense."

"Okay. That's all I had. I've gotta get to work."

"Of course. I'm glad you stopped by." Detective Myles got to his feet and escorted her to the elevator.

Amity hadn't expected him to get on with her, and in the close confines of the car, she thought he smelled good. Really good. When they arrived at the bottom floor, he stepped out and scanned the lobby. His eyes fell on a young woman, who Amity estimated to be in her late teens or early twenties.

"Miss Harmon?"

Oh, jeez. Is that Frank Harmon's daughter? Poor thing. What a terrible way to spend the holidays. Amity hurried to her car.

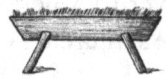

Without any word from Valerie and her calls going unanswered, Amity thought walking her dogs would help smooth out her emotional state. What she found was an argument. The nativity scene was still taped off, but Reverend Santos and an older man Amity didn't know stood nearby.

"Where is it?" The older man's arms were spread, palms up, and he accented each word with a bounce of his hands as he shouted at the minister.

"Eli, I told you. There were some expenses—I had to get an appliance repairman and a plumber out for the kitchen in the fellowship hall, then the garage door to the parsonage broke. I'll get you the receipts later."

"Funny, I never saw any repairmen at either the church or your house."

"Do you sit on your porch and watch all day?"

"No, but I'm out and about enough that I'm sure I'd see work vans."

A dark blue sedan pulled up in front of the men.

"I don't know what to tell you, Eli. The money's been spent, I'll get the receipts for you. And now my ride is here. Good evening. See you on Sunday." Reverend Santos got into the car.

The older man saw Amity as she and the dogs approached. He wagged a finger at her. "I wouldn't put any money in that collection plate if I were you, young lady. There's a fox in the henhouse, mark my words!" And with that, he stormed off.

After the walk was done and the dogs were fed, Amity called Phyllis. "Have you been over to Valerie's place just to make sure she isn't there? What if she's injured?"

"I've been there twice already. You want to go again?"

"I'll meet you there."

Phyllis used her key to open the front door. As they walked through the house, calling for Valerie, nothing looked out of place. It didn't look like there had been a struggle. There was also no sign of Valerie, and Amity even checked in all the closets. A nursery catalog lay open on the coffee table and a plant was circled—a hazelnut tree.

Valerie's profession was landscape design, so there was no reason she shouldn't have nursery catalogs.

Amity studied the page. She even took a photo with her phone.

"Hey, Phyllis? What zone are we in?"

"Zone? 9B, why?"

"Well, this bush she has circled says it's for zones 4-8. Would that grow in 9B?"

Phyllis rushed over to the coffee table and examined the catalog. "It *might*. But probably not a good bet. I can't imagine Valerie would intentionally plant a bush in someone's yard that was likely to die."

"I agree."

After another tour of the house and backyard, they both left.

Amity didn't feel like going home, so she drove around a little and ended up at the truck stop, because their restaurant was open 24/7. French fries were her comfort food, and she hadn't eaten dinner. While she waited to be seated, she noticed the young woman she'd seen at the police station, sitting at a booth with a young man.

Amity couldn't help eavesdropping.

"Ella, I think it's too soon to make any decisions."

"You don't get it. I'm not sad he's dead, not even a little. He wrecked my life. Good riddance."

"You don't mean that."

"Of course I do. I had enough in my college fund to get through a four-year degree. Barely, and at a public university, but still. And that's only because my grandmother left it to me last year. I was counting on that money. Dad thought he could double it or triple it or whatever. He took all the money and lost it on crypto. He wasn't even supposed to have access to it, but that guy at the bank somehow let him get his hands on it. I should sue them."

"I'm sure it was tough for him after your mom died, and he was trying to do the right thing."

"He fell for every get-rich-quick scheme that came around. That's how we lost the house and had to sell all of Mom's jewelry."

Her companion put his hands over hers. "I'm sorry."

"Meeting anyone, or is it just you?"

Amity jumped as the hostess reached for a menu.

"No. No, it's just me."

While she waited for her food, Amity studied the photo of the nursery magazine. Did it even mean anything? It was possible a client wanted one, even if it was likely to succumb to the heat and humidity.

A noise made her look up. Detective Myles waved at her from the hostess stand.

She beckoned for him to join her. When he got close to the table, she asked, "How's the case coming?"

"Early days." His eyes fell on the empty table. "You just get here?"

"I've already ordered, but have a seat. I'm sure she'll be back in a minute. You have any leads on Valerie?"

"I'm afraid not. I've been at an accounting firm getting cryptocurrency lessons this afternoon."

"You going to open an account, Detective Myles?"

He laughed. "Not anytime soon. I just thought it was interesting that the decedent had an address for a crypto wallet in his pocket and Mrs. Whittington's next-door neighbor owns a business that specializes in cryptocurrency. What are the odds of that?"

"Interesting." Wheels began to turn in Amity's head.

"I've probably said too much. But if you ever want to know about crypto, Hazelwood and Associates seems like the place to go."

Amity dropped her phone. "What did you say?"

"Hazelwood and Associates is the—"

"I think I know where Valerie is." She showed him the picture.

Strobing lights painted the sidewalk red and blue. Valerie, wrapped in a blanket, stood next to Phyllis on the sidewalk in front of Dorothy Whittington's next-door neighbor's house. She buried her head against her mother's shoulder as police wrestled a struggling man out of his house.

Amity just caught Valerie's whisper. "That's him. Miller Hazelwood. He was convinced I had some thumb drive. He said that Frank Hanson had it, and when he moved the body, it was gone. Since I found Hanson, I must have taken it." Valerie shook her head. "No idea what he was talking about. I was sure he was going to kill me."

A shout of "TASER! TASER! TASER!" grabbed their attention like a hand, and all three watched as Miller Hazelwood stiffened and fell like a plank into his manicured grass.

Amity winced. *That'll leave a mark.*

"What happened? How did he kidnap you?" Phyllis asked, rubbing Valerie's shoulders.

"He called and said he was Dorothy Whittington's neighbor, and he wanted to talk to me about Christmas lights. I told him my car was in the shop, and he said he'd come by my house. When he started ranting about the USB, I got scared. Then he destroyed my brand-new phone! I tried to leave a clue, but…."

"Phyllis and I were at your house, and I took a picture of your catalog. Detective Myles figured it out when I showed him."

"Well, speak of the devil." Phyllis turned her head toward an approaching figure.

"How are you doing, Valerie? EMTs should be here in a minute to check you out."

"Thank you, Detective Myles. I'm fine. Just hungry."

"You can thank Amity for showing me the clue you left. And, just so you know, we found a USB. It was under the ladder you dropped in the shed."

"MANGER SLAYER PLEADS GUILTY."

There wouldn't even be a trial.

Amity let the newspaper droop as she took a sip of her coffee and a big bite of her blueberry Danish. Bunny's Coffee and More typically had a constant stream of customers on a Saturday morning, but most took their purchases to go.

"This seat taken?"

She looked up to see Detective Myles. With messy hair and dressed in sweats, he looked like he had just come from the gym.

"N-no. Go ahead. I'm here by myself, Detective Myles." Amity hurriedly folded the paper.

"I'm off duty right now. Why don't you call me Finn?"

"O-okay, Finn. Do you come here often?" Amity cringed as soon as the words left her tongue.

"All the time," he said with a chuckle. "I see you're following the case." He tilted his head toward the newspaper lying on the table.

"Of course! My friend almost got killed."

Finn shook his head. "Poor Frank Hanson. Couldn't seem to win for losing."

"His daughter would probably agree with that."

Finn took a plastic bag of white powder and stirred it into his coffee. "He may have lost her college fund, but she's the sole beneficiary of his $150,000 life insurance policy."

Amity's brow had crinkled when Finn broke out the baggy.

He seemed to notice her confusion. "Post-workout protein powder."

"Ah," she said aloud. Her inner response was a whole-hearted *ewww*.

"I have no idea how Hanson dragged Reverend Santos into his crypto scheme. Guess the church had some deferred maintenance issues—he said he planned to use the payout for a new roof for the church."

"That makes it worse. Hanson was just out for himself, but the reverend was trying to support his flock."

"It was all fun and games until the crypto crashed through the floor, taking every cent of the original money with it. Don't know if the pastor was just embarrassed or hoping it would recover. He tried hiding the loss but ended up with an embezzlement charge."

"That doesn't seem fair." Amity took a dainty bite of her Danish.

"Well, he became a cooperating witness when it turned out that Miller Hazelwood, as church treasurer, was using the church's accounts to launder money for a cartel. Santos will get a reduced sentence, maybe even probation. The money that Hanson convinced Reverend Santos to invest was in a little used side account that turned out to be where Hazelwood was stashing the laundered money." He took a long drink of his coffee.

Amity sighed. "You just never know about people, do you?"

"Dogs." Finn raised his coffee, as if in a toast. "You can always trust dogs."

Amity's phone rang. "Hey, what's up?"

"Nothing much, Valerie. I was just fin—"

"That's great! Listen, Dorothy Whittington felt like such a local celebrity after being the neighbor of the Manger Slayer that she told all of her friends about my Christmas light business. You doing anything this afternoon?"

GREEN
By A. B. Richards

DETECTIVE Quetzel Cazares swore softly as one of her crutches thudded onto the carpet. In retrospect, she probably should have let the young uniform chase down the suspect. At least her quarry had been nice enough to break her fall when they'd tumbled off the parking garage.

Assigned to desk duty until her broken leg healed, she had been sent to the police library to scan documents. She had just finished processing a set of slides when an intern carried a banker's box down the stairs.

"Ready for the next one, Detective?" the dark-haired girl heaved the box onto the table.

"Ready or not, here it comes. Would you mind picking up my crutch?" Quetzel gestured to the floor.

Carla bent over and retrieved it.

"Thanks. So, what's in here? It's not more annual reports, is it?"

The intern laughed. "No. New stuff. So this guy, Tyrone Wilkins, joined the force when he got back from World War I. One day, he just disappeared. Nobody knows what happened to him. Anyway, his grandkids were cleaning out their parents' house and donated all his things. There's another three boxes upstairs."

Tyrone Wilkins. Haven't heard that name before. Wonder if the cold case group has looked into this? Quetzel struggled to her feet and reached for the lid. "Let's see what Mr. Wilkins has left us."

"I'm going over to the cafeteria for lunch. Can I bring you anything?"

"I'm good, thanks."

A gust of chilly air swirled into the room when Carla opened the door. December had finally extinguished the fiery summer that had lingered into the depths of autumn.

Quetzel hadn't been hungry until she stopped to think about food. She reached across the table for her lunch tote and had her own meal. Tyrone had waited this long; another fifteen minutes wouldn't hurt him.

Tyrone Wilkins leaned on the railing of the USS Hancock, staring as the coast of France expanded on the horizon.

"I reckon we outrun the U-boats." Wesley Faulkner was one of Tyrone's closest friends. The two of them, plus Andy, Nubs, and Cole, who were currently in their racks, had all marched into the army recruiter's office together three days after they'd graduated high school. "But I expect we could swim for it now, if one turned up."

Tyrone chuckled. "Farther than you think. Probably sharks, too."

"Well, you ain't nothin' but a rag, a bone, and a hank a hair. Shark'd spit you right out."

"Never been outta Harris County or the state of Texas, much less the US of A. What do you suppose French people are like?"

"Prob'ly like folks back home, just with a funny accent." Wes spat over the side of the ship. "Sarge said them French girls was awful pretty."

"Maybe. But I bet not a one of 'em can hold a candle to Eloise."

"Why dincha marry her before we left?"

Tyrone had thought about it. He was pretty sure she'd say 'yes.' But there wasn't time. Everything had happened so fast. "I swore to her I'd come back, and I aim to keep my promises."

Wes slid his hand along the railing. "I reckon just about ev-er-body's swore that."

Quetzel opened the lid and peered inside. Pushed against a long side of the box was a fancy container. The bottle appeared to be hand-blown glass that curved and twisted into intricate designs. The label said it was absinthe. She took a picture of it and loaded the record into the database.

Next, she lifted one lumpy envelope after another, until something shiny caught her eye.

She frowned at the flat, dark green glass bottle that rested at the bottom of the container. *What on Earth?*

It was heavier than she'd expected. She got a piece of printer paper and laid it on the desk, then carefully centered the bottle on top of it. She took a few photos with her phone, then used one of them for an online image-search. Within a minute, her screen filled with pictures of similar bottles.

Imperial Russian Army canteen. When this thing was freshly issued, it would have been sealed with a cork and had a canvas or leather cover with long straps attached for carrying.

World History class had been more than half a lifetime ago, and she remembered next to nothing about the War to End All Wars. It started with the darkly absurd assassination of Archduke Ferdinand, moved to deadly mud, both in Passchendaele and the blood-soaked trenches, and was finally ended by the flu.

She was afraid to know what stories the bottle could tell—she had nightmares enough already. For all the glamor of TV cop shows, working Homicide is a cumulative trauma. Unless you're a sociopath. She'd once worked with a detective who was. Arthur had a better clearance rate than average, probably because he could slip into the mind of a killer as easily as other people slipped into a warm bath. Sometimes, Quetzel envied his unperturbed sleep. Still, she was always wary of him. It was like having a pet wolf.

She opened one of the bulky envelopes and carefully slid the contents out. Some military medals. A silver ring with an inscription. A hammered brass spoon with the handle made from a .30-06 rifle bullet.

Quetzel laid the medals on the table, side-by-side. Purple Heart was easy to identify. She had to photograph and image-search the other two. One was a medallion of an angel carrying a sword and shield—that was the Inter Allied Victory Medal, and the other was a Citation Star, ancestor of the modern Silver Star.

Next, she examined the ring. Light for its size, so perhaps aluminum? The thickened, round pad at the top was shakily engraved with the word 'TWANC.' The internet had no suggestions as to its meaning. Was the 'C' an unfinished 'G?'

The bullet spoon was something else. The pointed tip had been split so the neck of the spoon could be inserted into it and then they were welded together. It was unlikely that the round was live, but she handled it gingerly all the same.

Yellowed, mud-stained playing cards, and a letter-sized envelope slid out of the next package, heavier than the first. Something large was wedged inside, so Quetzel reached in to free it. Her fingers wrapped around an odd-shaped metal object, and she nearly dropped the blocky Mauser pistol when it came into view. Curiously, the number '9' was carved into the handle and stained red.

"Hello? Sanchez?" Quetzel called up the staircase. "Got a gun down here."

Tyrone woke with a start.

Nubs was calling him from outside the abandoned French farmhouse. "Ty! Come out here!"

Wary of trickery, Tyrone nudged the man sleeping nearby. "Andy! Andy, get up. Nubs is callin' me. Krauts may be using him to lure us out. I'll go out the front, you go around the side and flank 'em. Just in case."

The two men tiptoed between the ragged survivors. Their 60-strong platoon had been winnowed down to eight in only three days, and the remains of the battalion were in a disorganized retreat, slogging through knee-deep mud on empty stomachs.

The moonless dark lay heavy on the ravaged countryside. Tyrone shuffled his feet through the sloppy ground to avoid stepping in big holes, even though he could barely feel his toes.

"Nubs!" he whisper-shouted into the gloom.

Not so much as a breath of air stirred. He couldn't see anyone. But Nubs' voice had sounded like it was just outside the window. *Where could he have gone?*

Naked trees stood watch over the house at the edge of this clearing in the depths of the Argonne Forest. About twenty yards out, the end of a cigarette glowed, a single red point in a sea of black. *Does the cig belong to Nubs or Cole? Both of them know better than to light up in the dark where they can be seen!* Wes didn't smoke, and the three of them were taking a shift of lookout duty.

Tyrone crept along, his ears straining to hear voices, hoping for them to have American accents.

"Whassat?" a voice near the dot of red hissed.

Wes? Tyrone hooted like an owl twice.

"Ty?" That was Cole.

Relief surged over Tyrone. He shuffled faster. A whippoorwill called behind him. That would be Andy.

"What are you doin' out here?" Wes' voice was raspy from thirst.

"Whadda ya mean? Nubs was at the window call—"

The farmhouse exploded, the shock wave knocking the five men to the ground ahead of the fireball that roared in its wake. Debris and shrapnel whistled past Tyrone as he curled his arms around his head, fully aware that luck was the only thing keeping him alive.

Someone started screaming. A man with his shirt ablaze was on his knees a few yards behind Tyrone.

Andy!

Ty rushed over and knocked him down, rolling his friend in the mud to smother the flames.

They followed the groans to the trees, where Cole, Nubs, and Wes had been hiding. Nubs and Wes had minor shrapnel wounds, but the flickering cigarette lighter revealed that Cole's leg was in bad shape. Tyrone used the strap from Cole's canteen as a makeshift tourniquet.

The tar-black night was fading to sooty grey on the horizon when Tyrone slunk to the blasted wreckage of the cottage on the off chance that any of the other three men had survived. There weren't enough remains to put together a whole man from the remaining fragments. Ty sighed and turned to go. A flash of silver caught his eye.

Underneath the shattered floorboards was a metal box about a foot long and perhaps ten inches wide, no thicker than a Bible. When he bent to pick it up, his sleeve pulled painfully on the scab forming over a jagged tear in his right forearm. His adrenaline had been so high that he hadn't even realized he'd been wounded.

He snagged the box and hurried back to his friends.

Quetzel watched as the firearms trainer from the pistol range removed the firing pin from the Mauser and put it into a bag with a number that matched the one on a cardboard circle that now dangled from a string looped through the trigger guard.

"Cool find." Sergeant Simms grinned at Quetzel. His dishwater-blond military flat top was nearly the same color as his skin. "Never seen one of these in the flesh."

The intern crossed her arms. "It looks like it came from a carnival or something, with that big red '9' carved into the handle. Are you sure it's a real gun?"

Quetzel had known Simms for over a decade and cringed as his jaw tightened. He didn't take well to having his knowledge or authority questioned.

Sergeant Sanchez, who was running the library project, stepped in before Simms had a chance to unload on Carla. "That gun's not common. It's very old. From World War I."

"If you say so."

Carla, Carla, Carla. You're on thin ice, girl.

Eyes narrowed, Simms looked up from putting the pistol back together. "Luger 9 mm was standard issue to German troops in the Great War. But they couldn't manufacture them fast enough, so the army made up the difference with Mausers. At the time, most of *them* took a 7.63 cartridge. But the Germans used 9 mm for the Lugers and wanted the Mausers to take the same ammo. That's why there's a '9' on there—to make sure they'd use the right bullets."

Well, that makes sense.

Simms picked up the reassembled gun and its pin and left to lock them in the secure storage area.

With a huff, Carla clomped back up the stairs.

"Find anything else good?" Sanchez leaned on the table where the envelopes from the box were spread out.

Quetzel did a quick show and tell.

Sanchez licked her lips. "There's some good shit in there. I think we can do a display in our timeline exhibit about how the global turmoil of that era had local effects. I'll get Carla on the research."

Her phone rang, and she hurried up the stairs. "Hey, LT… yeah…" The sergeant's voice faded as she turned down the hallway.

The letter-sized envelope still lay on the table. Metal clinked against metal as she picked it up. She frowned at four more aluminum 'TWANC' rings, copies of the first. *Why does the internet not know what this means?* She set them aside to be photographed and moved on to the next batch of artifacts.

It contained a fat stack of envelopes bound with a ribbon. She untied it and found that they were all addressed to Eloise Lambert. Must have been his sweetheart.

It seemed voyeuristic to read them, an intrusion into an intimate space. But victimology was crucial to solving murders, and the letters may contain some clues to his disappearance. Likewise, some tales of the war might explain things. Quetzel also wanted to handle the fragile paper as little as possible.

She lifted the lid of the scanner.

Tyrone barely remembered rigging a travois and taking turns dragging Cole along until they finally caught up with the rest of their battalion at Charlevaux Ravine. They were immediately sent to what passed for an infirmary, where their wounds were disinfected and stitched up. Cole's leg had to be amputated at the knee.

Wounded and starving, Ty, Nubs, and Wes joined the ragged survivors in keeping the enemy from overrunning their camp for another four days before relief showed up.

The afternoon before Cole and Andy were to be shipped to a hospital in England, the other three men sat around their cots. The Casualty Clearing Station was full-to-over-flowing, so no one paid them any mind. Still, Ty looked over both shoulders before he pulled the metal box from under his jacket.

"I found this… at that little house."

Wes scrunched his forehead. "Wassinit?"

"Don't know. Haven't opened it yet."

"What are ya waitin' for?" Cole shifted under his thin woolen blanket.

Tyrone struggled with the bent latch. Finally, the lid squeaked open. He lifted out an unopened, fanciful glass bottle of absinthe and passed it around for inspection.

Next came a cloth pouch filled with francs of various denominations.

After that, a small wooden box. An inlaid design in brass that could have been either fish scales or slate shingles framed a painting of a couple in old-fashioned clothes dancing out in a forest with people sitting around on rocks watching them. He opened the lid and a white porcelain ballerina popped up. A few tinny notes sounded, but not enough to recognize a tune. Tyrone didn't see a crank, but it was probably best not to wind it and draw attention to themselves. From the box, he retrieved a necklace with a large, faceted green stone pendant. He didn't think it was an emerald, but he was no jewelry expert. Four gold bangles and a silver pin with blue stones followed.

As the items came back, he tucked them into the box and set it on the floor.

"Now what?" Nubs grinned, eyeing the absinthe.

"You can't drink that stuff straight, ya dunce." Wes gave a half-laugh.

"So, I was thinkin'." Tyrone looked around. "Why don't we split up the money, then the other things, I can mail to my cousin back in Katy. He works at that new bank, and he can put it in a safe deposit box for us. When we all get home, we'll have that drink and decide what to do with the jewelry."

Andy squirmed under his bandages. Morphine had run out days ago. "I agree. Except for one thing. Tontine. All make it back, meet up and claim it. Else, last man standing gets it."

The implication that any of them might die here hung heavy in the air.

"Why a tontine?" Tyrone wrinkled his brow.

Andy's chest crackled as he pulled in a big breath. "Whoever lives longest probably needs it most."

"Ok. How do we draw it up?" Nubs glanced around at the men, his eyes falling on Tyrone.

"Lookit," Wes said. "One of them fellers shippin' out with you, with the broken leg and missin' arm? I got to talking to him. He's a lawyer. He'll know how."

Tyrone nodded. "You go scrounge some paper and ask him."

While Wes was gone, Tyrone counted out the money. It amounted to about 15 francs each. He put Wes' share back in the pouch.

Cole refused his portion, except for a silver two-franc coin. "Won't need French money in England."

"Keep mine, too." Andy mumbled. Sweat beaded on his forehead in spite of the chilly weather.

Solemnly, Tyrone redistributed their coins amongst the remaining three soldiers. When Wes returned half an hour later, he proudly held up a ragged sheet of paper with the tontine agreement. They each signed, and Ty placed the document in the metal box. Once he wrestled the lid closed, he reached into his pocket.

"I was watchin' some of the boys since we've been back, making all kinds of stuff with old shell casings and what not. One of 'em was using aluminum from a German nose cone to make rings. He showed me how to do it, and there's plenty of that junk laying around."

Tyrone handed each of the four an almost identical aluminum ring. The letters 'TWANC' were etched into the pad at the top.

"Whatdya think?" he looked from man to man. "May as well have a souvenir from our little jaunt to France."

Cole put his on his index finger. "I like it. But what does 'TWANC' mean?"

"It's our initials, blockhead." Wes rolled his eyes.

Nubs slowly twirled his between index finger and thumb. "We otta have them sent to you for the tontine box, if we don't make it."

The only sound was Andy's labored breathing.

Andy died of sepsis during the night from his infected burns. His ring was the first to be placed in the metal box the next morning. Tyrone put it in the music box with the other jewelry. He had been sure that the ballerina was completely white, but now her pointe shoes were pale green. He chalked it up to the poor light in the infirmary.

Cole traveled alone to England.

Quetzel had scanned about half of the love letters. She re-read one, after carefully tucking it into an acid-free sheet protector.

Oct 9, 1918

My Dearest Eloise:

We lost Andy last night.

Have you ever heard of the Argonne Forest? Sounds like a place from a fairy tale, but it is really from the worst-possible nightmare. We ran out of food and bullets while we were surrounded by krauts. If that wasn't enough, we were getting shelled by our own artillery! You know what saved us? A bird. A ridiculous, beautiful carrier pigeon. Even after getting shot, he made it back to HQ and they halted the friendly fire. In gratitude to him and his kin, I've sworn off dove hunting from now on.

We had holed up in an abandoned house to shelter from the cursed rain that has plagued us this entire campaign. Nubs, Cole, and Wes were on patrol while me, Andy and some other infantrymen tried to get some shut eye.

I'm not crazy. At least, not any more than anyone else in this Third Circle of Hell. But things have happened that I cannot explain. I was awakened by Nubs, whispering at the window, telling me to come outside. At first, I thought those sneaky Jerries were up to something, but I grabbed Andy, and we went to talk to him. We spotted the rest of the boys in the tree line, but before we could get there, the building was hit with a shell. We were all scuffed up—sad to say, Cole lost a leg. But Andy got burned. We all made it back to the ravine where the survivors were hunkered down, but they couldn't do much for him.

Now here's the thing: Nubs said he never came to the window. I don't know who, or what, woke me up. After Andy died, I'd gone out a little way from the camp to water the bushes. A pair of Huns snuck up on me in my vulnerable state, and I took a bullet to my left shoulder. Before they could fire a second round, the 307th turned up to liberate us. I was able to grab the Mauser out of Fritz's hand and shoot both those krauts dead.

The medics patched me up and I will be fine, so please do not worry for me. I am warm and dry in the infirmary as I write this letter, and pain notwithstanding, it is a pleasant change!

I have never put much stock in the supernatural, but events have conspired to give me the sense that I have a guardian angel.

I miss you more than words can describe, and I cannot wait to again be in your arms.

With all my love,
Tyrone

Statistically, most homicide victims are killed by someone they know, so Quetzel picked back through the newspaper clippings and made a note of Tyrone's four army buddies. *Had something caused a falling out between them after the War?*

Wesley Faulkner

Cole Harrison

Richard "Nubs" Nubeebuckus

Andrew Spinelli. *Well, not him. At least, not without a ouija board, anyway.*

The 'W' of Wesley and the 'C' of Cole stuck in her brain like grass burrs. Why were they significant?

Her crutch slid over again, knocking the envelope of rings to the floor and scattering them on the carpet.

As she struggled to pick them up, she went from swearing to laughing. Of course. Tyrone, Wesley, Andrew, Nubs, Cole. TWANC. *Well, I've solved one mystery, anyway.*

When Quetzel put the rings back in the envelope, she noticed a slip of paper. She unfolded the brittle find and spread it on the table, under the full glare of the fluorescent lights.

'Fox Brothers' Pawn and Loan' was printed in block lettering at the top. The faded handwritten words on the form were difficult to read, but as best she could tell, Tyrone had pawned something for $2 in October of 1922. A quick search showed her that Fox Brothers, located in the Freedman's Town section of the Fourth Ward, had been bought out by Gold Street Pawn in 1975, which had in turn been taken over by a national chain in 1998.

The building was protected as a historic site, with its own fancy bronze marker. Money-laden developers started trying to move into the ward shortly after the shop had changed hands and 'clean up' the historic area for well-heeled home buyers. Gentrification collided with community around the turn of the century, and Quetzel had a vague recollection of a huge protest happening in the early 2000s.

The alarm on Quetzel's phone rang. Time to wrap up for the day. As she updated the inventory spreadsheet and saved it, she made the decision to stop by the pawn shop—it was not terribly out of the way on her trek home. She snapped a photo of the receipt and packed up the box.

The yellow brick building hunched on Taft Street between West Dallas and Allen Parkway. 'Santa shops here for LESS!' in red and green paint was streaked across the plate-glass window, and the gaudy neon sign assured Quetzel that the shop was indeed open. The cowbell on the door jangled as she shoved it with her crutch and hobbled inside.

A middle-aged man with greying stubble looked up from behind the counter. "Help you find something?"

"I hope so. Do you still have records from 1923?" Quetzel's crutches creaked with every step on the uneven tile floor.

"1923! What?"

Quetzel flashed her badge. "Detective Cazares. Looking into a cold case. I know it's a long shot, but I thought there might be a chance you had the books somewhere."

He sucked his teeth. "It's possible. Nothing earlier than 1995 was put in the computer, though. There's a bunch of old file cabinets in the storage area, but I have no idea how far back they go. Never had any reason to look."

"You mind if I poke around?"

He tilted his head and pursed his lips together. After a few moments, he shrugged. "Normally, I'd say 'Come back with a warrant,' but 1923? Everybody's long dead. Who even cares anymore?"

"Thanks."

"Yeah. Merry Christmas. Come on. I'll show you where they are."

Quetzel followed the man into a dusty storage area. He flipped a switch and a bare lightbulb dangling from the ceiling flared to life.

"This is all the old stuff. Knock yourself out." He padded back down the narrow hallway.

Damned Bolsheviks. If not for them, he'd already be back home with Eloise. Cole and Nubs had shipped stateside months ago. Wes was in an outpost somewhere along the Trans-Siberian Railroad, trying to keep the bloodthirsty Cossacks and opportunistic Japanese from moving in on Russian territory during the political turmoil. General Graves had promised that as soon as the Czech Legion was extracted to Vladivostok, the American Expeditionary Force was on its way home.

Tyrone's hands were so cold he couldn't feel his Browning Automatic rifle. The only reason he was sure it was still there was because the weight of it made the strap dig into his bony shoulder. Even so, his gloved fingers were too stiff to fire it, should the need arise. It rarely got as low as twenty degrees, much less below, back home in Houston, but the icy fist of the Siberian winter held Vladivostok below negative twenty most days. And to think he had complained of the 90-degree summer heat just a few months earlier. Wishing he had a hit of that now, he stepped back into the train.

The inside of the car was not substantially warmer than the outside, but at least it was out of the wind. He'd ditched his US Army-issued aluminum canteen in favor of a glass one from the Russian White Army. Took longer for the water to freeze, especially with a shot of vodka mixed in. Tyrone had a sip—he barely noticed the alcohol anymore and wondered if that was good or bad.

He sighed and placed a hand on the center of his chest. The reassuring lump of metal and stone was still there. Tyrone had started wearing the necklace from the tontine box the day Andy died. He wasn't sure why he'd taken it before he posted the package back to the States. The green stone had invaded his dreams, and when he was awake, it intruded on his thoughts. Wearing it silenced its call. He knew it was completely unreasonable, but he had the feeling it was a talisman, keeping him safe.

Tyrone drank more water, then stoppered the canteen. He walked down the aisleway, the hollow eyes of the Czech Legionnaires who weren't sleeping fitfully met his as he passed. At the end of the Great War, they'd been caught in the crossfire of the Russian Revolution and were forced to fight their way through the Red Army to get back to their homeland—the shiny new Czechoslav Republic. New country, same war-ravaged land. *Good luck to 'em.*

A few of the battle-hardened soldiers had their families with them. A baby cried from near the back of the carriage and its mother sang softly to it.

His thoughts flew to Eloise. How she would be such a wonderful mother to their future children. Tyrone's arms ached to hold her.

He continued his patrol to the next car.

Quetzel coughed from the cloud of dust that puffed into the air when she pulled open a file drawer. This was the third one she'd tried. The old records had apparently been haphazardly dumped in the drawers, because if there was a rhyme or reason to this filing system, she couldn't see it. There were three or four ledger books for each year, but they weren't filed as a set, or even by year.

The very last book was wedged in the corner and difficult to retrieve. Quetzel almost gave up on it, but when she pried it loose, she was ecstatic to find that it contained records from August, September, and October 1922.

She thumbed through the pages until she got to October, then began reading the entries.

Finally! There was the listing on the second to last page:

#727348. 30 Oct 1922. Tyrone Wilkins, old music box with ballerina, $2

The $2 did not appear to have been paid back. *Was it because he disappeared before he could?* She took a photo of the ledger with her phone and checked the other page for additional Wilkins items. The music box was the only one.

Tyrone proposed to Eloise the day he returned home, September 18, 1919. Without hesitation, her answer was an enthusiastic 'Yes!'

Her father, however, was unsure, fearful that Tyrone's worst scars were the invisible kind.

By Thanksgiving, he had relented, and a December 21st wedding date was set.

While Eloise and her mother picked out bridesmaids and dresses, Tyrone chose groomsmen and planned the honeymoon.

Wes had a bad time of it on the Eastern Front and was still recuperating in a hospital in England. Cole and Nubs were automatic choices for the wedding party. Wes' cousin, Nelson, agreed to stand in for him.

Tyrone had just gotten off work as a patrol officer at the Houston Police Department and was in the middle of changing clothes to go to his wedding rehearsal.

The phone rang. He walked into the kitchen and picked it up.

"Hello?"

"Tyrone? This is Verla Harrison" Her voice was shaggy, as if she'd been crying.

Why would Cole's mother be calling? A cold chill curled around his spine. "Oh. It's nice to hear from you."

"I'm afraid it's not. Cole fell sick yesterday. Dr. Mayberry came out, said it was Spanish Flu and sent him off to the hospital." She sniffled. "Penny rode in with him, but now I'm scared for her and the baby."

"Oh. I'm so sorry to hear that. Listen, he was tough enough to get through the Great War. He's gotta be tough enough to get through this. Maybe Penny won't take sick. Aren't pregnant ladies immune to just about any illness? That's what my mother says, anyway."

"I sure hope Esther is right."

"Thank you for letting me know. Hang in there, Mrs. Harrison. Everything will be okay."

Verla started crying and hung up.

Everything was not okay. Cole died the next afternoon, and Penny was in the hospital instead of just visiting. It made for a somber wedding, and Tyrone pushed the honeymoon back a few days so he could be a pallbearer at Cole's funeral.

After the services, Nubs and Tyrone left together to deposit Cole's ring in the tontine box. Tyrone lifted the musical jewelry box and opened the lid. The ballerina's legs were now pale green, and her shoes had darkened to glass green.

"Hey, Nubs. Does this look any different to you?"

"What's that?"

"Ballerina."

Nubs shrugged. "Never really saw it up close. Looks like any other music box dancer to me." He extended his hand. "Lemme see."

Tyrone dropped Cole's ring inside and handed it over. Nubs felt around the bottom until he found the crank and gave it a few twists.

The ballerina twitched in a circle, her jerky movements unsettling. But the music was even worse. The metal insides must have warped, forcing a minor key on what seemed to be *O Holy Night*. At least Tyrone thought it was. Some of the notes were muffled, and some didn't play at all.

He cringed inwardly. "Probably nothing a little sewing machine oil wouldn't fix." But he doubted it.

Nubs closed the lid with a snap. "If I wind up with this thing, I'm gonna burn it."

The pawn slip seemed like a dead end. Even allowing for the differences between 1922 money and today's currency, $2 doesn't indicate a priceless antique worth killing for. There were a few more envelopes in the box, so Quetzel continued going through those.

The first one she opened had color photos of paintings of roses. She couldn't be sure if the artist was trying their hand at Impressionism, or just wasn't very good. Not for lack of practice—there were dozens of similar pieces. There was no indication of who painted them or why.

The next envelope contained fragile newspaper clippings. Quetzel smoothed each yellowed paper and tucked it into an acid-free sheet protector. There was an article about Eloise Wilkins' prize-winning roses. Her mother said the trick was coffee grounds. Three recipes—wacky cake, vinegar pie, and hot milk cake. Several articles about the opening of the Houston Zoo. A clipping with a photo of a gaunt Eloise standing with unfocused eyes by one of her rosebush paintings displayed on an easel. A third-place ribbon was clipped to the corner of the canvas. Delia Lambert—her mother—had entered the painting for her in the inaugural 1932 Houston Fatstock Show and Rodeo art contest. Eloise had died a few months after.

Quetzel was down to the last few envelopes.

Tyrone's shoulders drooped as Wes rocked back and forth on the front porch, picking at his left arm.

Betty's eyes fell on her brother, then Tyrone, tears sparkling in her lashes. "Wes don't talk to anybody but Daniel."

"Wes? Hey, Wes?" Tyrone tried again.

His friend's head turned, and he smiled at the empty bench to Tyrone's right. "Daniel! When did you get here?"

He paused, as if listening to a reply. "You know she won't tell me where it is."

"Can I help?" Tyrone leaned forward in his chair.

Wes just rocked, smiling at the settle.

His body had come home, but his mind stayed behind in the frozen tundra of Siberia. Tyrone had heard the story. They all had. Wes and his detachment were overrun by Red Army coming up the Trans-Siberian Railway.

He was the sole survivor of the skirmish. And that was only because one of his fellow soldiers, Daniel Moynahan, had fallen on top of him, concealing Wes from the ravaging Bolsheviks. Most of Daniel's head had been taken by machine gun fire, and the blood from his ruined face dripped down onto Wes until it gradually clotted and froze. For almost two days, he'd lain there, staring at the ragged mess that had once been his friend, until their relief showed up.

Wes was on top of the mass grave with the others when a soldier shoveling dirt on the bodies saw him blink. They medevacked him, and he was in the hospital for a long time, but he never spoke again. At least not to anyone living.

His sister and a few cousins took turns caring for him. Tyrone's police patrol beat led him past Wes' house, so most days he and his partner made time to check on his friend. For all the good it did.

It was a few days before Christmas, 1920, when Tyrone stopped by for the last time. An ambulance was parked out front. Betty and her mother stood holding each other and sobbing in the small yard.

Tyrone ran to them, dropping the presents he'd brought in the grass. "Betty? Mrs. Faulkner? What happened?"

Not meeting his eyes, Betty squeezed his hand and shook her head. Her mother wailed, and the sound of her cry reverberated deep within his soul.

Tyrone shoved down his emotions and raced to the porch. When he slowed to a walk to enter the house, he was met with two men carrying a stretcher. A figure covered in a sheet lay on the conveyance, dark blood stark against the white cotton, as the lurid stain seeped down the fabric from the top of the body.

Tom Ferguson, the Justice of the Peace, followed close behind, his face pale and drawn. He paused when he saw Tyrone.

"He finally found the gun. Don't know where he got the bullet. Betty swears there weren't any in the house."

At the funeral, Betty gave Tyrone the aluminum ring. TWANC. The third to go in the tontine box.

TWANC was down to TN. Tyrone was nervous about what he would find in the music box with this deposit, and he put it off for several days. When he finally made the trip, the ballerina's tutu was light green. Her feet and legs were dark.

Quetzel studied copies of the police reports from December 2, 1922, the night that Patrolman Tyrone Wilkins disappeared, and the continuing investigation.

Neighbors had reported being awakened by two gunshots, then the sound of a car roaring away.

Augustus Banks, the Wilkins' next-door neighbor, rushed out of his home and knocked on their door. It wasn't fully closed and came open. He found Delia Lambert in hysterics and her daughter, Eloise Lambert Wilkins in a catatonic state. Tyrone and Eloise's daughters, Beatrice and Belladonna, who are approximately eleven months of age, were fast asleep in their cribs. Tyrone was not at the residence, and Mrs. Lambert did not know where he was, only that he had had dinner with the family earlier and was reading the newspaper in the living room when she went to bed.

Mr. Banks alerted his wife to go and comfort Delia and her daughter. He got into his car and drove to the police station, as he thought nobody on the block had a telephone.

He returned with three officers approximately an hour later. They did not note any disturbances, aside from two bullet holes in the living room wall next to the door that leads into the kitchen. After ensuring that no miscreants were lurking on the property, the officers left. One of them was a friend of Tyrone's and asked where his dog Sergeant was. Delia reported that her son Homer had taken it to his home, so that Delia had fewer things to manage.

A photographer arrived at 10 AM the next morning and took a photograph of the bullet holes in the wall.

Investigators were unable to locate Tyrone or find any clues to his whereabouts. His wife remained in a catatonic state. She would occasionally mumble the word, 'green.' No one knew why or what it meant.

Quetzel frowned as she scanned and numbered the reports. She had questions, like how much time elapsed between the gunshots and the car leaving? Had Tyrone had any altercations with family members or neighbors? Was there gang activity in the area? But anyone who could answer them had been dead for decades.

She entered the records into the database, tucked the reports into their acid-free envelopes, and picked up the next item.

It was an old journal. *Surprised the family didn't want to keep this.* It belonged to one of the twins. The cover was tattered, but Quetzel thought she could make out the name 'Beatrice.' She read as she scanned it. About half the entries were teen angst related. Most of the rest were food-related—about how they grew their own vegetables because they didn't have enough money to buy them or traded with the neighbors for staples. Or what a treat it was when they went to Prince's Hamburgers for the girls' thirteenth birthday when it first opened in 1934.

There were a few nuggets of interest, though. Both girls were broken-hearted that their mother never recovered her faculties. Delia had often stayed over to help with the twins, and she moved in to care for them and Eloise after Tyrone vanished. Her daughter would often lie on the ground next to her rose garden until Delia had the idea to give her some paint and a canvas. Eloise painted picture after picture of the bright roses.

The girls had wanted to surprise Eloise with some new flowers, and a neighbor had given them some crinum lily bulbs. When Grandmother saw them digging in the flowerbed, she came unglued. Bella was truly terrified, and the old woman screamed that she would tan their hides if she ever caught them messing around in the rose bed again.

Beatrice was beyond frustrated that her mother never said anything but 'green,' and never interacted with her daughters in any way. Their grandmother guarded Eloise like she was Fort Knox, which didn't play well with the kind of social life the girls wanted. Although, during the Depression, 'social life' was open to interpretation.

Investigators at the time believed that the trauma of watching her husband being murdered and/or abducted put her in that catatonic state. How was green related to that? Did the killer wear a green shirt?

On the other hand, maybe her mind broke when *she* killed Tyrone. Quetzel had no clue about what was green, though.

Tyrone handed Nubs a cigar.

"What, I don't get two, since it's twins?" Nubs grinned at his friend.

"Two it is." Tyrone passed another stogie to his buddy.

The men stood on the front porch of Tyrone's house. The midwife was still inside with Eloise and her mother. Tyrone and Nubs had been banished out into the December twilight.

Nubs puffed his cigar. "December's stackin' up to be a pretty expensive month for you, what with your anniversary, two kids' birthday, and Christmas."

"Yeah. The 21st, 23rd, and 25th. Since they're in a single week, I might be able to save money and combine them into a single event—Birthversamas."

"If you do that, I hope you built Sergeant's doghouse big enough to hold you and him both."

Tyrone laughed. "You're probably right. Listen, about tomorrow…"

"I understand. The girls arrived a little earlier than you expected. I'll put the wreaths for Andy, Cole, and Wes out, don't worry." He tapped off the ashes. "I've been dreaming about them for the past few days. We're all still in school, then suddenly it switches to that house in Argonne, before the shell hit."

"It's that time of year. I mean, Andy had no hope of making it to December, but it almost seems like harvest season—first Cole, then Wes. You be real careful going home tonight. Prohibition be damned, there's enough booze in this city to pickle an elephant. In fact, if you want to stay over tonight—"

"With your mother-in-law and two brand new babies? No thank you."

Tyrone had fallen asleep on the couch and was awakened by someone knocking on the door. It took him a few moments to figure out where and when he was as he stumbled across the dark living room. He snapped on the porch light and turned the knob.

"Marsh?" Tyrone squinted in the sudden brightness at one of his fellow officers.

"Yeah. I thought you'd want to know. There was an accident. Some hooch hound hit a pedestrian."

"You woke me up to tell me that?"

"The pedestrian was Richard Nubeebuckus. Isn't he an old army buddy of yours?"

"He is. What hospital?"

"He didn't make it. I'm sorry."

Tyrone hung his head.

Tyrone went to the bank to pick up the metal box. It was all his now. The absinthe, the music box, the jewelry—everything. Tyrone wanted none of it. Not yet. Perhaps when they were old men who had lived good, long lives. Tyrone was too raw to feel dread. He jerked open the lid to drop the ring in.

This time, the ballerina's bodice and arms had turned light green. *Guess I'm the head, then.*

Quetzel rubbed her eyes. They were blurry from staring at the screen for hours. She had five pieces of paper in front of her. A copy of a handwritten note regarding the death of Andrew Spinelli during WWI, Cole Harrison's and Wesley Faulkner's death certificates, a newspaper clipping about Richard Nubeebuckus, and a tattered police report regarding the disappearance of Tyrone Wilkins.

Aside from Andy, they all died in December, on consecutive years: Spinelli 1918 in France of burns, Harrison 1919 of Spanish Flu. Faulkner 1920 of suicide; Nubeebuckus 1921 from an auto/pedestrian accident, and Wilkins disappeared in 1922.

Quetzel did not believe in coincidences, but she struggled to find a relationship. There seemed to be a pattern without a cause.

It was late October when Tyrone began dreaming of the dead. Each restless night, his brothers-in-arms waited for him at that little house in the Argonne Forest. They looked the same as they had before the shell hit. He was so happy to see them, but the sound! He clapped his hands over his ears, trying to block out the wretched, tinny music from the jewelry box. It was no good—the noise was *inside* his head. Nubs, Wes, Cole, and Andy all smiled at him. Tyrone screamed to wake himself. He sat up in bed, soaked in sweat, and clutching the green pendant he had put on and not taken off since the day Andy died.

Hadn't Nubs said he dreamed about the other three just days before he died? And hadn't all of them, save Andy, passed right before Christmas?

There was also the accursed music box. The little dancer changed with each death. What if he got rid of it? *Could it really be so simple?* Tyrone was not ready to go. How could he leave Eloise alone with two tiny girls? The thought of it broke his heart.

First thing in the morning, he emptied everything out of the jewelry box. Tyrone left early for work to give himself time to stop by the pawn shop.

"It's not in the best shape." Timothy Fox turned the box over in his hands.

Tyrone hoped he wouldn't crank it up and play the discordant tune. When Timothy opened the lid, Tyrone caught the reflection of the ballerina in the plate-glass window. She was white as bleached cotton. But when he looked straight at her, she was mostly green.

"Well, you know, I've got Christmas shopping. I'll take whatever you'll give me for it."

Timothy wound the crank, then winced at the result. "That can be fixed, I think. Two bucks."

"Done."

Tyrone hadn't felt so light-hearted since his girls had been born. It could be that getting the music box out of his house was all it took. He whistled as he walked his beat, and his partner asked if Eloise was pregnant again.

"Not yet," he'd replied with a wink.

He did not dream that night, nor the next month. But when December rolled around, the dreams returned in full force. After he screamed himself awake, he crept out of bed and made his way in the dark to the cabinet where he kept the metal box he'd found in that cursed forest. Seemed another lifetime ago instead of a mere four years.

Tyrone flipped on the light, yanked the long metal box out of its hiding place, and carried it to the table. When he opened it, he almost shouted. There was the wooden musical jewelry box, jammed in on top of the TWANC rings. *How? How did it get here? He still had the pawn slip—it could not have been redeemed.* Tyrone had to take the bottle of absinthe out to make space to wiggle the music box from its tight quarters.

He hurled the music box across the room as hard as he could.

It shattered against a doorframe and crashed to the hard-wood floor. A few twisted notes rose from the debris. Tyrone had the idea to stomp it into a thousand pieces.

The broken remains moved.

Tyrone stepped backward. *What the hell?*

The little green ballerina heaved herself out of the rubble and began dancing toward him. With each step, she got bigger, until she was almost as tall as Tyrone. Her legs had too many joints and there were flashes of other limbs. Too many limbs.

Tyrone continued backing up. "Stay away from me!" he hissed.

Still, she danced, closer and closer, in that disjointed, uncanny way, her petite smile growing into a malicious grin as she approached.

At last, she stopped. "Not how I expected this to work out, but I shall accept it."

"Get back!"

"Even after I saved your life?"

Tyrone scowled.

The ballerina opened her mouth and Nubs' voice came out. "Ty! Come out here!"

"No…." He shook his head rapidly. "Why would you save me *then*, only to kill me *now*?"

She unfurled ragged batlike wings with a *whoosh*. The neat bun on top of her head fell loose into long green tendrils that seemed to move of their own volition. "That… is complicated. You've heard that ridiculous tale about the Green Fairy that lives in the absinthe bottle? I have been bound to this wretched thing by my sister. She collected my belongings and the absinthe into a box and buried it under that abandoned house deep in the forest. But… what she didn't know was that I had hidden a tiny piece of my wing inside the ballerina. It was like having a little window on the world outside the bottle. But I needed power to escape. You were kind enough to carry me away from that dreadful wood. To places brimming with power for the taking."

Tyrone cursed under his breath.

"The first, the one you called Andy. He was not my doing."

The pendant became uncomfortably hot against Tyrone's chest.

"But he was just the kick start I needed. You kept it going." Her smile was unpleasantly wholesome.

"I don't understand."

"I *might* have lied to my sister about what my necklace does. It stores power, power I could use to pull myself, a little at a time, out of that horrible bottle. The stone drew energy from you as you wore it. And with each soul added—"

"My friends are inside this pendant?" Tyrone clasped the stone.

"Calm yourself. You're about to join them."

The fairy raised her hand, and green energy crackled around her fingers.

A floorboard creaked.

Slowly, the fairy's head turned... and turned... a full 180 degrees, until she was looking over her back at Eloise.

Eloise screamed. The babies began to cry in the other room.

Tyrone tried to take advantage of the distraction, but without even seeing him, she cast a bolt of magic.

It hit Tyrone in the chest and knocked him backward, his head striking the edge of a bookshelf. He collapsed to the floor, a pool of red spreading out beneath his hair like a rusty halo.

Ignoring Eloise, the fairy turned her face forward, then bent to take the pendant from around Tyrone's neck.

"No!" Eloise grabbed the first thing at hand and charged the Green Fairy.

She swung the bottle of absinthe at the fairy's head. Instead of striking with a crunch, it was more akin to hitting a pool of tar. The fairy's body rippled like a pond when a rock has been thrown in. She reached for Eloise, but her liquid arms flowed up toward the bottle. She roared in rage as she twisted and warped, and the glass sucked her completely inside.

Although he could see little but the ceiling, Tyrone heard the entire event from within the pendant.

"Eloise! Eloise, talk to me!"

"She can't hear you, man." Andy's voice, distorted, surrounded him.

Dawn had crept through the windows, and Eloise's mother opened the front door. She gasped and Tyrone was aware of chunky heels clapping against the hardwood.

"Eloise? Snap out of it." Delia must have seen Tyrone lying stiff and cold on the floor, his head surrounded by a jagged circle of dried blood. "My god! What have you done?"

Eloise did not respond, and her mother clacked off toward the girls' room.

It wasn't very long before the front door flew open. "Crap!" a male shouted.

Ah. Tyrone recognized his brother-in-law's voice. Homer was not a bad guy, but he wasn't the brightest bulb in the marquee.

Clattering from the kitchen made Tyrone believe that Eloise's mother was making breakfast for the girls.

"What happened?"

"How should I know? This is how I found them. She's just staring at the wall and he's dead as a doornail."

"Do you think *she* killed him?"

"Somebody did."

"Well, what do you want me to do, Mama?"

"We have to protect your sister. That means we've got to dispose of the body and clean up all that blood. You know what? Tyrone just dug up a flowerbed, so Eloise had a place for her roses. You can bury him in there."

"I'll get the spade."

"Not now! People will see you. We'll have to wait until dark. Wrap him up in a tarp."

"Are there any in the garage?"

"Where else would they keep them?" Delia paused. "Maybe we should fire a couple of bullets into the wall, so it seems Tyrone was taken by force."

"I can get Daddy's old .22 this evenin'."

"Good plan. And you'd better take that dog home with you. He'll dig up the whole flowerbed." She shook her head. "I've gotta feed these babies."

Quetzel studied her notes. Witnesses had been awoken by two gunshots around one AM. A car drove away in a hurry, leaving a traumatized Eloise and the twins alone in the house. No ransom note, and no trace of Tyrone was ever found. Investigators suspected that it was revenge by someone he'd arrested, but no recently released criminals matched up.

Whatever Eloise saw, it broke her. She remained mostly catatonic for the rest of her short life, occasionally uttering the word 'green.' Painted her rose garden obsessively.

Why? Why were those roses so important to her?

Quetzel typed in the address of Tyrone Wilkins' granddaughter's house into her internet browser. These nineteenth-century homes typically had large lots. People grew their own food. Fruit trees. Gardens. Chickens. Why not a goat or two? No HOAs back then. She switched to satellite view. There was a flowerbed in the center of the yard, and Quetzel estimated it to be eight to ten feet long and two to three feet wide. *Is this where the roses were?* Looks like something else is there now. A thick-bored live oak tree loomed directly behind the bed and closer to the fence. *Whole lot bigger than the one in the paintings.*

The grandma was obsessed with that bed. Was she protecting the roses because they were the only things that Eloise responded to? Or was something else going on?

She pulled out a copy of the single crime scene photo: two holes in the living room wall. The resolution was very poor by today's standards. It was the placement. That's what had been bothering her. They were too high. It was more like the shooter was aiming up, above people's heads.

Once you eliminate the impossible, whatever remains, no matter how improbable, must be the truth. No shit, Sherlock.

"Hey, Sanchez! I think I know where Tyrone Wilkins is."

Quetzel stood near the equipment operator as the drone pilot sent the robot in a grid pattern back and forth over the yard.

"Kinda looks like it's delivering pizza." She adjusted her knit hat.

"Yeah, a little." The operator stayed focused on the lines flowing across the small screen.

"What are you looking for?"

"A hyperbola."

"A 'U' shape?"

"No. That's a parabola. Hyperbola's two 'Cs' back-to-back."

Quetzel kept her eyes on the drone. When it finally made its approach to the flowerbed, she started peering at the screen. Some of the lines began sloping down, then up.

The operator nodded to Quetzel. "Looks like we got a hit."

Sergeant Sanchez sat in a chair next to Quetzel, studying the Medical Examiner's report. "So, was it murder?"

"At this point, it's impossible to tell. Somebody could have struck him, but he also could have fallen and hit his head."

"If it was an accident, why would they have buried him in the backyard instead of calling the cops? He *was* an officer."

"Perhaps they didn't *know* what happened? His wife had a nervous breakdown around that time. Relatives might have thought she did it. Maybe she did." Quetzel shrugged. "At least he's had a proper burial now."

"What's that?" Sergeant Sanchez pointed to a faceted green stone pendant on a tarnished silver chain that lay on the table near the bankers box.

"He was wearing it when he died. It got sent off to the lab, but he'd been buried in the family plot by the time it came back. Granddaughter brought it by. I meant to ask if we had a jewelry box or something like it to put this in."

Sergeant Sanchez shouted up at the loft. "Carla!"

Her face appeared over the railing. "Yes?"

"Would you go in my office and grab one of those little flat boxes for me?"

"Okay."

A few minutes later, the intern came down the stairs with two sizes of cardboard container. "This what you wanted?"

Quetzel started to get up and snagged her orthopedic boot on the leg of her chair. She caught herself, but the pendant went flying. It landed hard on the tile floor in an explosion of green dust.

"No! No, please. Don't put us in a box!" If only they could hear him.

Tyrone had been so hopeful. When he'd finally been dug up from that god-awful flowerbed, he wanted more than anything for a relative to take the necklace and wear it around. He wanted to see the sun. Something. Anything besides dirt. In the over one-hundred years the TWANC had been trapped in the stone, they'd discussed everything on Earth there was to discuss. As much as he loved them, he felt he was starting to lose his mind.

The pendant suddenly became airborne. When it clattered to the hard floor, it cracked. It was a tiny crack, but it was enough!

Tyrone, Wes, Andy, Nubs, and Cole flew out of the green stone without a backward glance. Tyrone was so enthralled with his newfound freedom that he almost failed to notice the doorway. Beyond it was a dark tunnel surrounded by spinning lights. But in front of it...

"Eloise!" Fast as thought, he was at her side.

She threw her arms around his neck and their energies merged in one ecstatic moment. "It's time, Ty. It's finally time."

Hand in hand, they turned and walked down that long tunnel.

The detective swore. "I am so sorry."

A sound like a muffled scream came from somewhere behind her, and she scanned the room. "Did you hear that?"

"Eh. I'm sure it's just the cadets doing something outside." Sergeant Sanchez scooped up the pendant. "It's got a crack in it now, but it isn't broken." She started toward the table.

"What's that?" Carla pointed to the ornate bottle in the box.

"Absinthe, from World War I or earlier," Quetzel answered.

Carla held out the boxes to Sergeant Sanchez. She chose one and placed the necklace inside, then wrote on the lid what it contained.

Carla picked up the absinthe and raised it up to the light. "Is it supposed to have glitter?"

Quetzel looked at it. "That bottle has a lot of shaped surfaces. I'm sure it's only light refracting off the different planes of the glass."

The intern swirled the absinthe around. "How about we crack this open just to see what's in there?"

If you enjoyed this book, please consider leaving a review at your favorite book site. Reviews help other readers find and enjoy new books!

To explore more content from Artemis Greenleaf, A.B. Richards, and Holly Dey, please visit BlackMareBooks.com